Duffle Bag Bitches 2

By

Alicia Howard

1

CH

Duffle Bag Bitches 2

Duffle Bag Bitches 2

© Revised 2016

by

Alicia C. Howard Presents

Saint Louis, Mo

Chapter 1

Things are in full swing; music jumping, the girls talking shit, and teasing Shannon who is sitting on Zane's lap. Dallas on a business call even Dizzy is in chill mode playing on the game in the warehouse. Jay and Jasmine talking like they lost each other for years.

Things looking really good from where Zane sits. They have some cool music playing but Zane needs to hear that new *Yo Gotti.*

"Get up boo." Zane says Shannon.

"Where you going? You leaving?" she asks.

"Not without you, going to my car to grab a CD." He told her.

She moves out his way so he could go the door. Dallas called after him, "See she already got you in a thong. You got to explain your movements and shit." He loves to talk shit with his people.

"Don't worry about mine nigga. I got this!" Zane pops his collar.

"Tell him daddy." Shannon strokes his ego.

"See you hear that?" Zane points to her.

"Man take your ass to your car. Talk shit when you come back in." Dallas laughs.

Zane is laughing as he steps out of the door. He is halfway to his car when a 45 touches his temple a voice he doesn't know says "Nigga move and you're dead!"

"Man look I don't know who you are, nor why you have a death wish. Whomever sending you here doesn't have your best interest at heart. I promise you if you walk into this warehouse with this gun to my head. You will not walk out alive." Zane is cool as a fan he talks to the gunman.

"Who the fuck you think you are nigga? Smooth talking as if you're not about to die!" The man says. His voice is shaky that let Zane know he is certified. Something deeper move him to come here today.

"Dude if you were a killer I would already be dead. That tells me a lot about you. State your piece man causes you're not about this life." Zane waiting for the right time to reach for his hammer. He about to lay this lame ass nigga down.

The man knows that Zane is right because he isn't a killer. He has never killed anyone nor plan to today. He knows that shit on his home front been very different. He wants some answers that's all. Zane is getting pissed by the second.

He sees that dude is deep in thought he reached for his .45 then steps away aim at him.

"Nigga speak now or never speak again in life." Zane doesn't really give a fuck what this nigga has to say. There is something in the man's eyes screaming don't shoot me.

The two men heard a familiar voice say, "Don't worry about me and mines. I'm going to check on my baby. He's been out here too long for me." Shannon says as they gave her shit about Zane.

She steps out of the doorway seeing the two men. Zane has fire in his eyes. Shannon knows she better speak now before shit gets real crazy.

"W-w-what are you doing here Korey?" she chokes on her words.

Zane doesn't look her way, his heart wonders if this is one of her little niggas. If so, he better be ready to die because he isn't getting her back. He never looks away from the nigga he asked. "You know this bitch ass nigga?" Zane is hot as hell.

"Yes baby, it's not what you think. Put the gun down!" Shannon doesn't want to piss him off more than he already is.

"Well what fuck is it then? This nigga came gunning for me! You're gonna have to tell me something better that or this hammer gonna do the talking around this muthafucka." Zane huffs.

Shannon begins to slowly walk over him. Once she is close to him she places her hand on his back. He melts and lowering the hammer. Zane looks at her face seeing that a tear is sliding down her cheek. "Why you crying? You love this nigga?" The question hurt him leaving his mouth.

"Yeah I do, he's my brother in law." Shannon says him.

"What the hell is she talking about man?" Zane asks Korey.

"Jasmine is my wife. I followed her to find out what she has become more important than her family lately." Korey says him.

Zane shakes his head extending his hand to Korey. When Korey grabs it Zane pulls him in for an embrace. "We are family my dude. Never put a gun to my head again expecting to live. Now let's walk through that door get the answers you came here for." Zane feels for the man not knowing the lifestyle his wife is living.

The trio walks back into the noisy warehouse. Everyone is laughing, drinking, and having a good talking about Mack's silly ass. The man will be missed because he is hilarious. Jasmine and Jay are glad their back together the two were tipsy.

This is the reason that Jasmine thought her eyes were playing tricks on her.

Chapter 2

"Zane who is your friend?" Dallas asks knowing that Zane know that you don't bring anyone but family to the warehouse. He is hoping that good pussy Shannon putting on the nigga hasn't fucked up the business side of his brain.

"You should ask Jasmine." Zane says to him.

"Jasmine?" Dallas calls her name.

"He's my husband Dallas." She stands up looking at her husband seeing the hurt in his eyes. Jasmine walks over to him once she got close his words pierced her like a bullet. "Don't come too close I have a gun." He says coldly.

"What?" Jasmine knows he is mad but damn.

"Don't act like you don't fucking understand why I'm pissed Jasmine. I work my ass off for you and all four of our kids. I deal with your mouth and fucking attitude. Now I find you in a fucking warehouse with these hustlers!

You want to walk up on me like my mind isn't saying kill this bitch? The only reason you are still alive is because my heart says I love her yet them children love her more." Korey says.

14

Duffle Bag Bitches 2

Jay and Shannon are crying because they both honor and loves the man Korey is. Jasmine often acts as if she doesn't value what she has, it's what every woman wants. Now here this man is willing to risk his life not knowing what he walking into.

Dallas is shocked that this woman is married. If he known beforehand she had a family she wouldn't be a part of his team. Jasmine had too much to lose. Recently he worried about the love growing between Shannon and Zane. Yet something tells him that they are the modern day Bonnie & Clyde.

Jasmine doesn't know what to say. Dallas senses it so he decided to speak.

"Man first off let me introduce myself. I am Dallas." Korey looks at him like who gives a fuck. He isn't a killer but he isn't a bitch either. If his hand is forced, he could do it.

"I dig it, you don't give a fuck, I get that. You want to know what the fuck your wife is doing here. She works for me I didn't know she was married. If I had known, she was married I would have never let her get down with my team.

Now that she's with us I can't let her walk because she's knows too much. You can come here anytime you need to check up on your wife or get down if you want. That's all I can say my man. I am sorry." Dallas states his peace hoping the man understands where he is coming from.

There is also a part of Dallas that doesn't give a fuck. If the nigga was pulling his weight. His wife wouldn't have felt the need to get money. That may not true though. Some woman greedy, wanting too much, some just never seem to get enough.

"What you a hooker?" The words taste foul leaving Korey's mouth but he had to ask.

Jasmine slaps him "No nigga!" She is hurt beyond words that he thought that. Not to mention asking in a room full of people.

"This shit better is than my soap operas. Hell I am glad I got out today. If shit like this pops off all the time I will be here every day." Dizzy laughs.

"Not now nigga!" Dallas yells at him. Dizzy still laughing causing Zane to shake his head at the him.

"Jasmine don't put your hands on me anymore! You don't get a pass right now." Korey is dead ass serious.

"Can you come over here? Sit for a minute." Dallas needs to make him understand his wife's job.

"I don't feel like sitting plus I don't know you. So if you got something to say speak nigga." Korey is getting angrier by the second. He is ready to leave without his wife take his kids and never look back.

"Cool family we will do this your way." Dallas let him slide with the flip shit that came out of his mouth. If he had a wife, she had been on this bullshit he would feel some type of way too.

Chapter 3

"Your wife is a Duffle Bag Bitch. They are a part of my crew Duffle Bag Boys. We rob D-boys; mostly the ones that floss that paper too hard. I didn't make her get down with this life. Jasmine was already doing this with her crew Shannon, Jay, and Nisha.

When I saw how good they were I wanted them on my team. No one here is fucking or trying to fuck your wife fam. That's my word." Dallas isn't in the mood for this drama. He planned to have a laid back day.

"You rob people? Where the money?" Korey ask because he hasn't seen much change in their lifestyle.

Jasmine hand him the fifty-thousand-dollar check stating, "I got this today. I got another seventy-five hundred in the bank. Dallas put another fifty thousand in a trust fund because he doesn't want us doing this for the rest of our lives." She hopes this makes him feel better but she knows that money doesn't move him.

Korey laughs, "This a nice profit may I ask since you been down with this team has anyone on lost their life?"

Jasmine wasn't ready for that question.

"Yes Mack." Jasmine states.

"Where is he?" Korey asks.

"Dead." Jasmine states.

"I know that! Where is he? Did his family bury him? Did any of y'all crew make it to the funeral? Did you all leave him for dead?" he wants to hear what she has to say.

"No! He got shot when we were in another state. He died in the getaway car before the timer blew it up." Jasmine words cut the whole crew in a major way. It could have been any of them.

"Oh is that right? Who here got enough heart to come bring me this fifty-thousand-dollar ass check. Tell me my wife has been shot and blown up in the back of some fucking car?" Korey looks around the room for Dallas.

"I hope Dallas since you already told me that she can't get out because she knows too much. I don't like this shit; I am damn sure not working with y'all. Jasmine grown she can do what she wants. I am content that she not fucking anyone here. Still not happy with the life she has chosen to live though.

I will tell you Dallas one thing; the day this one die know that I am coming here looking for you. I am willing to live and die for my wife. No matter how stupid she is at times, I love her. You can take that how you want to boss." Korey wants to kill Dallas but knows this isn't the time to act on it.

He hands Jasmine the check back, "Good job gangsta don't forget you're a wife and mother first." Korey walks out of the warehouse with Jasmine on his heels. She hell on wheels but she isn't a fool.

Jasmine knows what she has, she's not going to let anything stand in the way of that.

Dallas wonders what kind of drama this would bring to his circle. Zane could read his thoughts, "No D! Let that shit be. That man has a right to go hard for his family. If you can't understand that you don't understand shit.

"You're right Zane. My thought out of order forgive me lord." He states. Dallas is a good dude but the devil won't let him go at times. Zane is the angel placed in this crazy ass man's world to balance him out.

Jay and Shannon runs out the door behind Jasmine. They know that she will need them. They headed home to clear their mind about what had taken place. Nisha was still on cloud nine from all the bullshit Dallas fed her about following his rules for her own protection. She was still sitting at his desk when Zane said "Nisha I think your ride is about to leave you." She smiled.

"It's cool I'll stay here and chill with Dallas if he doesn't mind." She smiled at Dallas.

"The pleasure is all mine." Dallas needed his dick sucked so if she wanted to stay that's what she would be doing.

"Aye Dizzy let shake this camp my nigga." Zane got up to go.

"Yeah nigga I'm worn out. I've been out too late already." Dizzy fussed.

Zane laughed at the nigga thinking this fool a certified killer with a bedtime. That shit was too funny.

Chapter 4

Jasmine tries to make Korey feel where she is coming from but he isn't hearing her. He would have left her ass if he could. Korey loves his wife too damn much to do something like that. He just wants her to understand that this is dangerous game she playing. Knowing his wife, he knows that he isn't going to be able to get her to stop.

Korey knows Dallas said that she couldn't quit but he doesn't give a fuck about none of that. If Dallas had to lay down to get his wife out of this shit, he could make it happen. He looks at his wife asking, "So you're a killer? A Duffle Bag Bitch?" He shakes his head.

"Yeah I am." Jasmine couldn't lie to him anymore.

"Why?" he needs to know.

"Because I am sick of this sorry ass life we live. I want to give my family more than what the hood has shown us." She fusses at him folding her arms across her chest.

"I thought that was my job to get my family out the hood." The man in him is hurt that his wife wants to do his job.

"It our job Korey; plus, you're a square. You would have never done this." Jasmine hates that she said that but it's the truth.

"Damn I am a square." He laughs.

"Yes! That's why I married you because you don't act like these crazy ass thugs."

"So you're the thug of this family?" Korey asks.

"Yes! I always will be." Jasmine isn't going give in he knows it.

They went home talked about a way to make the best of the cards life has dealt them. There is no turning back from

the decisions that has already been

made.

Shannon decides to take a ride around the hood in her purple on black Monte Carlo. It isn't a new boy like the hood is riding nowadays but its funky. She has that muthafucka tricked out. Shannon candy purple paint on the exterior, black flash show car interior, with ace alloys black machined with purple stripes.

She is riding up Broadway when she spots Laura arguing with a nigga. The nigga is yelling and talking shit. Shannon almost passed her up until she read Laura's license plate that read Dallas#1. He has twenty girls all their plates had his name; the numbers are different. She sees that Laura seems to be crying. Shannon makes a U-turn in the middle of traffic. She parks her car facing Laura's Shannon knows if the police see her they would have something to say but she would deal with that then.

As she exits the car she reached under the seat for the .380 that she kept with her at all times. Shannon steps out the ride walking up on the duo that hadn't seen her stop. Shannon begin to speed up when she sees the nigga has his hand raise like he is about to hit Laura.

"Hey Laura!" Shannon makes her presence known.

"Shannon?" She has met her once but isn't sure it's really her.

"Yeah that's who I be." Shannon says as she looks at the nigga "And you are?" she asks.

"Bitch my name doesn't fuckin matter! Who the fuck I am is someone this bitch owe money." He barks.

"Did you just call me a bitch?" Shannon steps to him.

"Yeah I did! What the fuck you feeling?" He asked.

"Nothing! That's a turn on boo." She states he looks at her like she is crazy.

"Girl you need to take your little sexy ass on somewhere. You don't have shit to do with this right here." He tells her.

"Actually I do." She informs him.

"How the hell you think so?" he getting pissed with her.

"She belongs to my boss," Shannon states.

"Belongs? Boss? Who your boss?" He is lost at the moment.

Shannon looks at Laura wondering why this man doesn't know who she works for. After today the world would know. "Does name Dallas ring a bell with you my nigga?" She knows it does by the look in his eyes as she points to plates on the car.

"D-D-Dallas yeah I know that name ma." he stutters.

"I thought you would. This woman you're talking to belongs to him. Whatever she owes you I think you should take it up with him. This shit you doing right here almost got you killed today." Shannon so smooth with her shit it scares dude that a woman could be so cold.

"Look baby this hoe gets her nose dirty. All I want it my fucking thousand dollars that she owes me, we can be done with." He talks like he is calling the shots.

Shannon hands the nigga a stack "There it's done!" she states.

He looks at this woman shocked as shit that she is holding that kind of money. While he is out here hurting. He hassling hookers to pay for shit they couldn't fucking afford. Hell he needs to meet Dallas.

"Hey ma my name is Roc I need to meet Dallas and speak with him." He tells Shannon.

"I know you would want to speak to Dallas. Give me your number I'll have him call you." She assures him.

"What the fuck you need to talk to him for muthafucka? She paid you go on with your life." Roc looks at Laura as the sick dope fiend she is. He walks away from her back to his car.

"Laura shut the fuck up cause your ass is in the hot seat. Now you owe me a thousand dollars. Please trust I am not gonna hassle you like that nigga Roc is. I am going to give you a set fucking date. You better have my fucking money that day or you're dead. I will have Dallas's approval to put your ass down." She doesn't see fire in Shannon eyes; she sees ice that is worse.

"Shannon we family!" Laura yells as Shannon walks away from her.

"Bitch we are nothing because you don't respect yourself or your family name! You're nothing to me." She says to her.

"I will have your money by that date." Laura knows Shannon doesn't play any games.

"Indeed!" Shannon tells her as she drives off.

Chapter 5

Zane has been calling Shannon's phone for the last forty-five minutes. He is pissed that she isn't picking up. "*What the hell could be keeping her?*" he wonders. His phone rings her name came across the screen. He doesn't want to pick up because he is so pissed but he does anyway, "What the fuck you want?"

Shannon looks at the phone hanging up because she just knows she dialed the wrong number. She tosses the phone on the seat heading to Zane's house. She barely takes the time to park the car. Then climbs the stairs two at a time to see what bitch in there with him. She has her .380 with her plans to use it on him and whatever bitch he has with him.

Shannon knocks at the door he opens it without even asking who it is. When Zane opens the door he staring down the barrel of the gun he smiles. "You come to kill me?" He so sexy.

"Yeah along with whatever bitch in here. That got you talking reckless on the fucking phone to me!" She barks.

Zane loves the fire that she has. It always makes his dick hard he isn't about to let her win like that. "You should have answers the fucking phone. When I called your ass a thousand times. Now you want to be grown and shit." He fusses.

"Want to be grown? Muthafucka I am grown! You don't even know why I couldn't pick up the phone. While you talking shit; if a bitch in here I am killing you and her ass flat out." She pushes pass him walking into the apartment.

"You the only bitch in here! So tell me why you didn't pick up the fucking phone?" He wants to slap the shit out of her at that point.

"Damn right! I am the only bitch up in this muthafucka. You better know it!" Shannon tucks her gun in the small of her back satisfied no one else is there.

Zane shakes his head laughing. "Since you the head bitch in charge why you didn't take my call Shannon?"

"I was cruising through the hood spot some nigga roughing Laura up and shit. I parked to check shit out, see what dude's issue is with her. Come to find out this hoe owes this man a band for some blow. She got from him a few weeks back. I paid him, he went on about his way. Saying he would like to speak with

Dallas. I took his number then told Laura she got a week to pay me my money or she dead." Shannon sit down on the couch lighting a kush blunt.

Zane hates that Shannon had so much G in her at times. He wants to see her act like a lady. "Baby why did you even stop? You don't know that nigga he could have fucked both of y'all up. You should have called me, Dizzy, or Dallas love." Zane says.

"Fuck that! So you saying I got to have a dick to handle shit?" She is pissed.

"No baby that's not what I am saying. I just want you to be safe." He lowers his head hating that she is a part of his crew.

"I am safe as long as I keep this heat with me." She pulls it out the small of her back.

"Put that shit away girl come fuck me!"

She walked over to him, "Ooooooh can we be nasty?" she purrs. That's so sexy to him because sex is the only thing that calms her down most of the time.

Zane licks her lips, "How nasty you want to be boo?" he asks in a sexy baritone voice.

"I don't want to be nasty. I want you to have me singing lullabies." Shannon smiles at him.

Zane knows what she meant he hit play on the stereo. "*We Can Get It On*" by Yo Gotti ft. Ciara belts from the speakers. Zane slams Shannon onto the bed asking "You really want this?" His sexy blue eyes have her frozen she just nods her head yes.

The beat drops the room got really hot. "*Mmmmhmmm*" Shannon moans as

Duffle Bag Bitches 2

Zane move his body to the music. For a thug he could dance his ass off; even if Shannon is the only person that knows. Yo Gotti drops the hook,

And we can get it on

Close your eyes shawty gone make a wish

You never met a

Nigga like this

And we can get it on "I know yo pain - all

the shit you been through I

Just wanna see ya dreams come true

And we can get it on

Right here right now back seat

And we ain't gotta make it to the suite and

I'mma go strong

And I'mma hit it hard like the beat

guaranteed to

Put dat ass to sleep and have ya like

Shannon jumps off the bed into his arms wrapping her legs around his waist. Zane is still dancing with her hanging off of him ripping his wife beater to lick and bite his chest.

He two steps her to the bed "We can get on," he sings with the music.

"Zane stop playing! Give it to me you know I love when you dance." She whines her pussy soaking wet and aching for him to touch it.

"Shut up! You my bitch I can make you do whatever I want!" Zane know she likes for niggas to talk rough to her.

"Oooohhhhhh daddy touch me please." She begs.

Chapter 6

Zane climbs on top of her still bobbing to the beat of Yo Gotti. He kissed her lips sliding his tongue in her mouth to allow their tongues dance. He licks down her neck then in between her breasts. Zane loves breasts even though Shannon's are small it doesn't matter to him. A breast is a breast.

He suckles at each nipple as she moaned, "*Zane it's dripping wet daddy.*"

He stops sucking her nipple for a moment. "Baby don't rush greatness; I will find out in a minute!" Zane begin to suck her nipples again as she laughs throws her head back enjoying the love making session.

Zane works his way from her nipples to lick inside her navel allowing his tongue to follow her happy trail to her happy place. He smiles when he got there because it's as wet as Shannon promised it would be. She doesn't know it but this is what hooked him. That she stays as wet as the Niagara Falls.

Zane parts her pussy lips with his tongue. The juice from this woman glazed his tongue like a honey bun would. Shannon is going crazy as he teases her. She hates and loves it, "Oooohhhhhh I wish you would stop teasing and deep sea dive in this pussy. Make your tongue dance in this pussy daddy." Shannon knows he loves to be called daddy.

Zane opens her pussy placing his whole mouth over it. He begins to suck Zane could feel the juices sliding down his throat as he sucks her dry. Shannon is trying to get away from him Zane has a lock on her ass. *"Oooohhhhhh aggggrrrrrhhh noooooooooooooooo plllllllllllllllllllllllllease let me go Zane."*

The only response she got is the slurping and sucking he is doing. Her body begins to jerk as she screams at the top of her lungs. Zane know that she planned on getting some dick but he can tell by the volume of her voice she isn't gone last.

"Ooooooh yes baby you the best! I can't take no more; oooohhhhhh please let me go." Shannon begs with tears in her eyes. Cum is spraying into Zane mouth he drinking every drop. As he drinks he begins to count in his head ten, nine, eight, seven, six, five. Shannon passed out once he reached the number five.

She blacked out he let her tough ass go smiling. Zane loves the fact that he has this skill most women never know until it happened. Shannon is out for the count Zane licks his lips dancing out the room.

Shannon sleeps for about forty-five minutes. She wakes up pissed because she knows what happened to her and she couldn't stop it. She doesn't like that at all; she has an issue with things that control her. Shannon jumps out of the bed naked looking for Zane.

She finds him on the sofa sitting up sleeping Shannon smiles. She walks over to him pulling his dick from his boxers. She knows that Zane wouldn't wake up until she is sucking on him because he such a heavy sleeper.

She lowers her body down to the floor between his legs. Shannon licks his shaft causing him to move a little bit but not wake up. She begins to suck and blow his dick; at first it was just the head. When she was to ready to wake him up she swallows him whole.

"*Whaaaattt the fuck!*" his eyes pops open to see Shannon staring him in the eyes. He loves a woman that would look at you while giving head.

Zane thinks it's the sexiest shit ever. Shannon is doing the damn thing. Zane is so glad that she would be his wife

soon. *"Damn girl you already got the ring!*

What you what you working so hard for

now?" He wants to scream like a bitch

but the boss in him made him talk shit.

Shannon know that she is putting it

on his ass. He is trying to play it cool but

she kept slurping and sucking him like

he is a super *Blow Pop*. That nigga can't

keep his cool. Zane begin to bitch, *"Babe*

alright yooooou fucking got me! I am sorry

for how I did you but pleassssse just come

sit on this muthafucka." He begs for two

reasons. One is because she about to

make a him cum. Secondly because he wants her to have his baby.

Shannon is cool with the request because she is pissed more about not getting the dick early before she passed out. She climbs on top of him just like he asks her. As she kisses him she slid down that hard steel Zane moans, *"Dammmmn girl... this my pussy for real?"* Shannon has this nigga hooked.

"Is it?" Shannon teases him because she knows that he would get mad.

"Shannon don't do that shit!" Zane will get pisses thinking about another nigga hitting it.

"Babbbbbbyyyy...." she began to ride him *"Why would I give anyone this pussy when you treat it so gooooood?"* Shannon drops it down on him. The two begin humping and breathing like two wild beasts in heat. The sex is insane between them.

They came so hard they just knew that heart attacks would shortly follow. To their surprise they both just fell into small comas of love. Shannon is on top of Zane he is still inside of her as they sleep.

Chapter 7

Jay has been home for a month now. She even dating this new little tender name Q. He is crazy about her wants all her time. Jay isn't sure if he is going be able to handle her lifestyle only time will tell. She really digging this man.

Q stands about five foot five with cocoa brown skin, husky frame yet he well built, easy on the eyes but too bossy at times. That is something that bothers Jay a lot because even in her line of work she isn't a person that enjoyed confrontation.

Duffle Bag Bitches 2

Jay would rather everyone be happy. She loves the time she is spending with Q but her mother on the other hand isn't so wild about it. Jay is her angel She wants the best for Jay but sometimes she too overbearing as well.

She would call Jay's phone so much at different times of the night. That Q thought it's a man that she keeps ignoring. Yet it's only her mother.

Jay has spent the last few nights at Q's place her mother is pissed blowing up Jay's phone causing Q to become angry.

"That is not your fucking mother Jay!" Q barks because the phone has gone off ten time at three in the morning.

"Yes the hell it is! Now go back to sleep I will see her when I get home later today." Jay is half asleep.

"If you got a nigga Jay! Pease tell me now because I am a Scorpio man our feeling isn't to be fucking played with! Do you understand that?" Q schooling her on who he was.

"Q you told me this shit before! I am sick of hearing it all fucking ready! I am a Cancer woman I don't think a bitch on this planet loves as hard as we do. At the rate you're going I don't think you will be finding that out!" She is pissed now that she is out of the bed on her feet.

Jay had enough of everybody bossing her around. She is a good person; never asks for much then love and understanding. Yet the people that come into her life wants to use her or control her. She not about that life anymore. At the moment she feels fuck Q and her mother; it's about her now.

"Baby, baby wait hold on! I'm wrong. it's just that I really like you. I don't want to be hurt. You feel me?" Q protests her leaving but by the looks of things it isn't working tonight.

"Whatever dude I am out of here! I'm not in the mood to be rational about what the hell you're talking about at this fucking moment. I am sleepy so I am going somewhere where no one will get on my fucking nerves!" Jay yells at him.

Jay heads for the door he has a sad look in his eyes, "Don't do this Jay for real!" She wants to give in but isn't willing to this time.

"What do you want from me Q? Never mind it doesn't matter I will call you later." Jay left his place because she knows if she stays to listen to what he wants from her they would end up having amazing sex. He would have won again. Not this time; Jay has a point to prove, not just to him but her mother was also in for a rude awaking.

Jay hops in her ride weeks ago she trades in her truck no she has a 745 Benz; all black everything. Only people that know her well would know that it's her because the plate reads *Jatavia.* That is her government name not many people know her by it.

She is cruising thinking about get a hotel room for a few days. So she could

get away from the madness that her
mother and man brings to her life. Jay
thought about heading over to Jasmine's
place but the house is still on shaky
grounds so she passed. She has enough
bullshit of her fucking own to deal with.

Jay knows that Shannon is at
Zane's place whenever her daughter is
with her father. That's a no go for sure,
she loves Nisha but doesn't really fuck
with her on that level. The hotel looks to
be the best thing smoking.

Jay pulls up the Moonrise Hotel.
One of the baddest places in the city
limits. It sits in the heart of the city but

most people don't even know what the hell it is. It's in the Delmar Loop, secondly its expensive; about three hundred dollars a night.

That's one of the things Jay loves about herself. Price doesn't matter to her if she wants it. Jay going to get it, she walks into the beautiful lobby the clerk looks sleepy.

"Do you have any rooms tonight?" Jay asks her.

"Why of course we do! How long you will be staying with us?" She sizes Jay up thinking the young woman is out of her league coming into the hotel.

"A week." Jay says her as her phone begin to ring.

"That will be eighteen hundred dollars with taxes." She smiles expecting Jay to curse her out like most people do when they hear the price.

Jay hands her two thousand dollars saying "I've got to take this call let me know when my key ready." The clerk looks like a damn fool. She mad as hell because she isn't in the mood to do any work.

"Sure thing Ma'am." She smiles doing what is expected of her.

Chapter 8

Dallas has called Jay's line a few times but its four thirty in the damn morning. She doesn't know what is in the air today. However, she sleepy as hell.

"What up Dallas? I know we not on the move again until Friday. So what's the word?" Its Monday what does he want at four in the damn morning?

"Girl who are you talking to?" Dallas always jokes around too much.

"Dallas I have had a long nigh baby. A bitch sleepy! Why are you bothering me?" she whines.

69

Dallas has a soft spot for Jay. Even though no matter what he says nor promised she won't be his woman. He fell for her the moment he came to St. Louis five years ago. She was working in a Starbucks he needed something strong to wake him up.

When he laid eyes on her the coffee was no longer needed. He tried to get at her but she isn't feeling it. Then told him since he was new in town that they could be friends but nothing more. Five years later her word is still her bond.

"Jay for real this business. I got this bitch Laura in my office talking about

70

Shannon hustling her for money. Some nigga name Roc rough her up today. I know Shannon but she can't try to double pimp my girl.

She free to find her own hoe if that's what she wants to do but mine are of limits." He fusses.

"The bitch is lying," Jay says.

"I know Shannon your dawg and all but..." Dallas is cut off again.

"The bitch is lying." Jay stands on that.

"One hour." Dallas lets Jay know that's all the time she has to prove her theory.

"Thirty minutes is all I need don't let the bitch out your sight." Jay informs him.

"Deal!" Dallas hangs up.

Shannon's phone is ringing off the hook. She wonders who the hell it could be calling at five in the morning. Shannon already let Zane know that she made it home. He was a little upset with her because he wanted her to stay the night. She couldn't because her daughter is being dropped off at eight am. Shannon doesn't want her fat ass baby daddy all in her business.

She grabs the phone off the nightstand "What is it?" Shannon doesn't give a fuck who it is on the other end. All she knows is it's too early for a phone call.

"Get up meet me at Dallas's now." Jay says.

"Why? We don't move until Friday." Shannon has been fucked greatly then had to drive all the way home. She doesn't want to go to Dallas's place.

"Laura!" Jay says.

"I will see you in ten minutes."

Shannon know that she is about to have a long day.

Dallas is informed that Shannon heading his way. He wants to see how Laura would respond to the news.

"That is Jay calling to tell me that Shannon will be here shortly. She has to make a quick stop first." Dallas says to Laura.

"What kind of stop?" Laura is nervous. She knows that she should have just paid Shannon her money. Be done with this shit unfortunately her drug habit is barely allowing her to make the

ten bands a month. That Dallas requires
the girls to make. He keeps five thousand
the other five thousand goes to the girls.
Two thousand of the five he took went
into a trust for each girl. Dallas is far
from a greedy man.

"I am not sure but she is on the
way." Dallas watches her bite at her nails
which isn't allowed. She rubs in her hair
repeatedly; another violation. Dallas
doesn't play about his women's
appearances. To make money your
presence must speak money.

If you look like a streetwalker you
will make a few hundred dollars. If you

portray a call girl you will make a few thousand. Then there is the elite that you take to formal dinners dates, their parents' house if you're gay, some of his women eating good playing wife for these fanboys, awards show, etc.

Those hoes will make a few million. That's what Dallas strives for; the million dollar bitches. At the moment Laura is looking like a two-dollar street walker. Dallas is wondering about her lately. She has always been very thick but at her last two weigh ins she is fifteen pounds lighter each time.

In a little over two months she has lost thirty pounds. Dallas know that she is on drugs; sometimes he like for people to hang themselves. That way he doesn't have to be the bad guy.

Chapter 9

Shannon arrives about five minutes after Jay who made it to Dallas's place by seven am. Shannon walks in with fire in her eyes. She has a nigga that Dallas had never seen before in his life but looks so familiar with her. Dallas know that man has to hold some important information for Shannon to bring him along.

"Ms. Zane glad you could join us." Dallas teases. Even when shit is crazy the man still finds a reason to smile.

"Cut the bullshit Dallas. I am mad as hell and sleepy so let's talk." Shannon barks.

"Laura is one of my favorite girls." Dallas lies. Jay laughs at how full of shit he could be at times.

"It that right?" Shannon has to laugh because Dallas is on his bullshit this morning.

"Yeah she is and it seems that you've been hassling her for money," Dallas calls for Laura. She enters the room looking loss when she sees Roc standing next to Shannon she wants to pass out and die.

"Really? Is that right? Hassling her for money? If anything I gave the bitch money! I will let my new friend talk for me." Shannon steps over to the sofa where Jay sat.

"You are?" Dallas isn't friendly with niggas; especially strange niggas.

"Roc my dude glad to meet you." He a cheerful nigga.

"Too bad I can't say the same. How do you fit in to all this shit I am dealing with? I got a bad bitch in the back waiting for me. so I don't want to be here all day." Dallas has become tired already.

"I feel you my nigga never keep a bad bitch waiting. If she nasty she going start without you." Roc is so serious but Shannon and Jay laughs at him anyway.

"I agree so let's get a move on." Dallas shake his head at Shannon and Jay.

"Shannon saved your girl Laura's ass. She on that white girl, owed me a thousand dollars for two months I had to get at her. Shannon peeps it stepped in, paid the debt like it wasn't shit. Now I don't know what took place after I got my money. I told Shannon to take my number down because I need to holla at you about a few business things." He spills the beans.

"They lying! Shannon fucking that dude that's why he saying all this." Dallas slaps the shit out of her causing a tooth to fall out.

"No they not, Shannon fucking Zane." Dallas said that because Laura always wanted Zane. He wouldn't have her because of the line of work she is in.

"Dallas!" Laura cries as if someone cared.

"You fired!" Dallas isn't going to kill her; he had too much love for her. She used to be his bottom bitch.

"Where will I go Dallas?" She cries some more.

"I don't care! I just want you far away from me." Dallas knew all the time she was lying. He was prepared for the walk of shame she would have to take. Dallas gave her a check for a hundred thousand dollars. It was all the money from her trust that she had built up.

Laura's eyes lit up when she sees the check that he had given her. Now she is on her bullshit, "I will gladly take this start me a new life." As she talks as Shannon gets up heading for the door.

"Shannon I will give you that little thousand dollars. I am tired of this bullshit life anyway." She Laura is feeling herself.

"You look tired; you should get some sleep." *BOOM*

The noise caused every eye in the room to blink, they all reopen their eye except for Laura's. Shannon hit her dead between the eyes.

"Shannnnnnoonnnn!" Dallas yelled yells as she holds the smoking gun.

"What?" She looks at him.

"Nobody told you to shoot her!" Dallas barks.

"Sure you did! You said death is the only way out! Since she was on her way out that was my que to send her home" Shannon hunches her shoulders.

"Go home Shannon." Dallas know this hell demon needs rest.

"Cool I'm sleepy anyways. Roc you coming?" Shannon waves the gun.

"No boo I will take a cab; I don't trust you." He is serious as hell.

"I understand; I don't trust me either." She smiles going home.

Shannon is heading home just when the phone begins to ring. She doesn't know the number its showing all zeros. She picks up, *"You have a collect call from Nisha."* The operator says. Shannon can't believe her fucking ears.

She hit five to take the call, "Nisha why?" Shannon is pissed.

"Girl it ain't shit but a DWI. I just need five thousand to get out." She says like its five dollars.

"Alright Nisha where you at? Jasmine and I will pick you up." Shannon is not in the mood.

"Cool sis." Nisha hangs up.

Shannon went to pick up Jasmine because she lives for this type of shit. Bailing people out is fun to her mostly because she is nosey.

Chapter 10

As they ride to the county, "Girl what the hell is she locked up for anyway?" Jasmine asks.

"DWI." Shannon isn't in the mood for the third degree.

"DWI! What the fuck is she stupid or something?" Jasmine always wants to run shit that has nothing to do with her.

"I don't know and I don't care. I just want to get this shit done." Shannon is nonchalant.

"Bitch you make me sick you never have anything to say about shit." Jasmine fusses at her.

"I don't because I know you can't control grown people." Shannon schools her.

"I don't care if I can control them or not. I am going let it be known how I feel about the situation." Jasmine rolls her neck folding her arms.

"That's the thing; no one gives a fuck how you feel." Shannon parks the car exiting to get Nisha's ass out.

"Bitch fuck you I don't know why I came with your stupid ass." Jasmine is pissed.

"Because your nosey bitch." Shannon says.

It takes an hour and a half to get Nisha processed out. By this time Shannon is starving and missed her daughter drop off. She knows whenever she picks her up she is going to have a lot of shit to deal with.

Nisha finally get released she walks out the place smiling. The trio heads back to the car. As always Jasmine has to open her damn mouth.

"Nisha you need to grow the fuck up. Stop playing games with your life." Jasmine hates this girl at times, and her brother even more for having kids with her. Despite Nisha's immature ways she takes damn good care of her kids though.

"Bitch mind your business! I just spoke on this before we fucking got out of the car." Shannon isn't in the mood for Jasmine's shit. She doesn't know why she always picking her ass up; sister or not.

"I am not talking to you so shut the fuck up!" Jasmine barks. Nisha never mumbled a word.

"If you want a ride home you gonna kill this shit now." Shannon looks at her ass for the answer.

Jasmine looks around at where she was. Clayton; she doesn't fuck around with the county especially not this part right here. Around here the only thing that matters is money, from the looks of her skin. They would assume she doesn't have any.

She decides to bite the bullet this time for her ride home. Jasmine jumps in the car without saying a word. The ride home is quiet until they pulled in front of Nisha's mother's house. She was about to exit when Shannon asks, "Where is my money?"

"Aww bitch I got you! We family I know it ain't like that." Nisha acts like she wants to play games.

"Yeah we family so I will give you a few days. I want my money by the time we head out for New York." Shannon informs her.

"I got you boo. It's nothing. I am just tired as hell don't feel like going to the bank." Jasmine looks at her as if she is speaking Chinese.

"I can feel that." Shannon let her get out hitting a U-turn in the middle of the street. She yells out the window as Nisha was walking up the steps. "FYI I killed Laura today because she owed me a thousand dollars and she was a liar. If you think, I am bullshitting call Dallas."

"What the fuck that mean?" Nisha is pissed behind the statement.

"I know you a liar so I hope you have my money by Friday or you gonna be a dead liar too." Shannon drives away heading to take Jasmine home.

The car pulls in front of Jasmine's house. Shannon looks at her, "Can believe this bitch Nisha?" she asks.

"I'm minding my damn business!" Jasmine states as she hopped out of the whip laughing.

"Bitch!" Shannon yelled knowing it is time for her to sleep.

Shannon arrives at the crib about to unlock her door when it opens for her. She is shocked to find Zane standing there holding her baby daughter.

"What the hell is this about?" Shannon asks knowing that she had left the baby with her dad a little too long.

"I was parked outside waiting for you when he came. He was banging on the door calling your name. Then started calling you names around this baby." Zane is pissed.

"So he just gave her to you? Not knowing who the fuck you are? That sorry bastard going to die." She is heading back out the door when Zane grabs her.

"Yes he gave her to me. I told him that I was your husband." he laughs.

"Why the fuck would you do that? Zane we are not married. Now this nigga is going be tripping about keeping her. When it's time for me to do my job." Shannon is stressing.

"Fuck that bitch nigga he gave this beautiful little girl to a fucking stranger. just because he said he is married to her mother! He sorry never deserved her or you." Zane is a man on every level.

"Zane I love you but..." Shannon says but he cut her off.

"You do?" Zane has been waiting for her to say that. He still holding the baby. She is rubbing the waves on his head.

"I do what?'" Shannon got loss for a minute.

"Love me?" Zane heartbeat is so loud a deaf man could hear it.

"Yes but I got a daughter and baby daddy drama. This is too much to put on your plate. You are you used to being single not being part of a family." Shannon fusses as she shakes her head.

He pulls out a box that read Cartier he hands it to her. She opened it inside is a platinum ring set with brilliant-cut diamonds, a center emerald-cut 5 carat diamond. Shannon looks at the ring then back at Zane as if he is crazy.

He could tell by her eyes that she about to make her mouth say no. Nonetheless he isn't taking no for answer.

"I know Shannon we just met. I have never done none of this with a woman. You are right; I am used to being a bachelor. Yet two pretty woman makes me want to be a family man.

Be my wife teach me what it's like to have family? I never had a family even as a kid. My own mother never even loved me. Shannon you say you love me; make me know it.

Shannon is speechless until Jailah her three-year-old daughter says, "Say yes mommy." She smiles when Zane

looks at her in shocked.

"Hi five miss lady!" Zane and Jailah

gave each other five.

Shannon laughs at them teaming

up on her already. She smiles saying, "I

can't think of a better man to marry." She

gave him a kiss feeling like a queen.

Chapter 11

Shannon brought Roc to Dallas but she doesn't know what she has delivered to her boss. Dallas can't believe the news this man brings to him. He needs someone to be there with him. Jay informed him that she will be tied up all day. Dallas isn't in the mood for Shannon's crazy ass.

He calls Jasmine to meet him at St. Mary's Hospital. Dallas know she is the best one for this news. She would play it cool because she is laid back that way. Dallas hears her husband fussing in the background. He is hoping that he doesn't have to make that nigga disappear.

Dallas is in the parking lot in an all-black Range Rover looking like a boss. Roc is sitting with him hoping the news he brings will get him a spot in the family. Jasmine pulls up in her undercover car that she keeps hidden from her husband.

Korey wondered how she could afford a Lexus. Well he knows now but he still isn't on the wagon yet so she keeps it hidden not too far from her house.

Roc meet Jay and Shannon but when he saw sees Jasmine his heart skipped a beat. He wants her at all cost. She walks over to the car with over-sized shades, a red from fitted t-shirt that read "Bitch Nigga Shut Up!", skin tight skinny jeans that hugs her body just right with red and black pumps. She is banging Roc has to have her.

Dallas stepped out from the car looking fly in the black with white stripes Adidas outfit, all black Ken Griffey's with the white/black Portland fitted cap. He is fresh to death Jasmine thought as she hugs him. If she wasn't married this nigga would be her man no matter who she has to step on.

"Why we here baby?" Jasmine asks Dallas.

"My man Roc here says he got something that we might want to see." Dallas informs her.

Jasmine looks at Roc he looks real familiar to her but she can't put her finger on it. "Nice to meet you love." Jasmine extends her hand to him.

Roc grabs it kissing her hand, "The pleasure is all mine." Dallas laughs shaking his head. Jasmine pulls her had away wiping the kiss onto the back of her pants. Roc knew his change with her are slim to none. He not tight about it because bad bitches have the right to pick and choose. They head to the main entrance of St. Mary's Hospital located at 6420 Clayton Road in Richmond Heights, MO. Dallas doesn't live that far from here because he owns a house in Chesterfield, MO.

"Boy bring your ass on! Show us what the hell you talking about. So I can get back home to my husband and four children." Jasmine strolls off on his ass knowing that she had left him with his mouth open.

They enter the hospital Roc walks up to the desk clerk who know him.

"Hey Rockwell. How are you today? I didn't think you were going make it." She smiles.

"Yes ma'am. I am running a little late. I had to pick up some family today." Roc says as if he driving.

"Well that's great! New faces and voices might help; go right on up." she hands them all visitor passes.

They took the elevator to the fourth floor. After a short walk down the hall they stop at the door reading Malcolm Smith. The name doesn't ring a bell to Jasmine. Dallas is frozen like a deer in headlights.

"Man! What kind of fuck games are you playing?" Dallas caught Jasmine off guard. She has never heard Dallas raise his voice.

"This is not a game! Are you coming?" Roc asks him.

"What the hell is going on here?" Jasmine fusses at the two men.

"Yeah we coming, come on Jasmine." Dallas grabs her arm because he needs her strength right now.

They walked in the room looking at all the tubes running through this a body. The beeping machines doesn't make the man laying in the bed unrecognizable. "Is that really him?" Jasmine walks over to the bed to touch the body.

"Yeah that's him." Roc told her.

"How? I watched the car blow up with him in it." Jasmine rubs his hand. As a single tear slid down her face.

"Mack is my big brother I follow him on every trip that he goes on. We know the rules of the war zone. Leave the fallen soldier to die; but I told my bother that I would never let that happen to him. As long as I was living." Roc told them. He is Mack aunt son she had him a little while

after she got custody of Mack. Roc
doesn't deal with his mother much these
days.

"It wasn't like that Roc we never
wanted to leave him but we had…"
Dallas's heart hurt looking at Mack laying
the bed. He doesn't look like he is in any
pain. Mack looked as if he is asleep.

"It's ok Mack know what this game
is about when he got down with your
team. No one can drag a wounded or
dead man along. I know your squad loves
him. They were ordered to leave him
where he got hit but they didn't.

They took him far as they could. I followed every step of the way. I got my brother to safety before the car blew up." Roc is proud of himself Dallas is impressed with his skills.

"How long has he been in the coma?" Jasmine asks now sitting at his side.

"Two months his body is healed. If he wakes up, he can go home but he has woken up yet; but he will." Roc says as if he is God himself.

"How do you know that he will wake up?" Dallas asks.

"God raises the dead all the time this no different!" Roc is confident in his savoir. Dallas is glad that he has the faith.

"Keep the faith man but I have to get out of here." Dallas doesn't know how to take all of this in.

"I understand man I just thought you would like to know he is alive." Roc says.

"Respect." Dallas says heading for the door with Jasmine in towing.

Chapter 12

The news blows Jasmine and Dallas away as they left the hospital. It caused Dallas's mind to respect life and other things. Jasmine breaks the silence as they walk to the car. "Wow can you believe that Mack alive?" she asks.

"No I can't we're going to keep this between us. We don't want to get everyone all happy then he passes." Dallas has a point.

"Yeah you right. I am known for running my mouth this is one that I will keep to myself for the sake of others. Especially my sister, she loves that man."

"Yeah she did I thought for a minute he was going to steal her from Zane." Dallas laughs.

"That crazy ass boy would have never made it!" Jasmine is right about that.

"I think you right about that!" Dallas smiles at her.

"Well I got to go home and feed my family. I will catch you later." Jasmine kisses him on the cheek heading to her car.

She walks to the hot pink Lexus she as she opens the driver side door she hears, "Your husband's a lucky man. If you ever want to get out of this game, I will close my eyes let you walk away." Dallas wishes he known that she was married beforehand.

"Glad to know that I will keep that in mind. We leaving Friday to make another come up. FYI it's not many nine to five that will feed, and clothe four kids nor keep a roof over their head. Don't worry about my husband he will get used to this." Jasmine states more so hoping.

"I am not worried about that nigga; I am worried about you." Dallas winks as she enters her car and drove off.

Jay knows that she has two day left before it was time to make a move. She had to get her shit it in order. She calls Q to see if he could meet her at this apartment she is looking at. It's time for her to be the woman that she is behind closed doors.

It's time to bring her to the light for the world to see and respect; especially her mother. She treats Jay too much like a child it's time for all that to come to a stop. Jay loves her more than anything in the world. Yet she wants her mother to see her as the woman she is.

Duffle Bag Bitches 2

Q pulls up in record time. He hadn't seen Jay since the morning her mother and he got on her damn nerves. He wasn't sure if he was going to get the chance to see her again. She wasn't taking his calls. When she called today he jumped at the chance to make things right with her.

He knows she is a good woman that he would not let slip away! They were at The Clayton on the Park which offers luxury high-rise apartment living in Clayton, Missouri. The luxury apartments boast walls to wall, floor to ceiling windows with twenty-three floors of amazing city views, granite countertops and designer fixtures. Residents experience unparalleled service and amenities such as a building concierge, valet laundry service, on-site spa, twenty four-hour fitness center, and rooftop lounge water feature.

Jay known that her first home would be the shit. She wasn't sure that it was going to be this fucking fire. She got the keys yesterday Jay decided to show it to Q before she finished it. She needs to talk to him on a really serious level.

"Whose place is this?" Q asked Jay.

"Mines!" She looks at him waiting for a response.

He looks at her like she is crazy, "Really? I thought you lived with your mother?"

"I did but it's time for me to become a woman. Women don't live with their mothers. They call their own fucking shots you dig?"

"I do. This is a big shot place you got here. Can you afford this? What do you do for a living?" Q asks.

"I take money and live well." Jay schools him.

"I bet you do." Q laughed at what he thought was a joke but he would learn one day.

"Q I brought you here because I want to know what this relationship we're developing is." Jay is not in the mood to sugar coat shit.

"I want you baby! I want to be in your world!" He is so sincere in his words but does he really mean them Jay wonders.

"Really?" Jay asks because she doesn't have time to play games. She needs someone that is going to be real.

"Yes I don't know how to make you believe me!" Q is kind of confused with this woman cause no one ever made him feel like she does.

"Trust me and move in with me. That will make me yours. My word is my bond." She is barking orders a part of Q loves it.

"Moving in? I don't know Jay." Q is ready for all that.

"It's now or never." Jay looks at the ringing phone then back to him "You going to make your choice because I got to take this call?" Its Shannon calling.

"I will move in Jay but I am not moving out. So we have to work out our ups and downs. You need to plan on becoming my wife in a few years." Q states.

"Yeah ok." Jay walks away thing he is talking shit.

Chapter 13

Shannon called all the girls to meet her at Mike Shannon Steak and Seafood. The girls aren't hungry but all agreed to meet for drinks. Shannon has taken Jailah to her mother's house. Zane went home to get some rest because Jailah wore him out. He loved every minute of it plans to take her shopping tomorrow. Since they will be heading to New York on Friday morning.

The girls don't know what the hell they are meeting for. They know how the game goes by now, they agree because it would be nice to catch up on the happenings of the crew.

Nisha, Jasmine, and Jay are already there waiting when Shannon arrival shining as bright as Christmas lights in mid-spring. She takes a seat they all staring at her wondering what the hell she so fucking happy for.

"What's good bitches? Did y'all miss me?" Shannon asks her voice matching the smile on her face.

"What the hell you so happy for?" Jay asks.

"Damn I can't come see my people with a fucking smile on my face?" Shannon asks.

"No!" Jasmine and Nisha agrees which shocked the shit out of both of them.

Jay begin to scream the people in the restaurant are looking at her like she as if she crazy as hell. Jasmine and Nisha are wondering what the hell is wrong with crazy. Jay covers her mouth pointing to Shannon's hand.

Shannon never moved she looks over the menu as if nothing is happening. When Jasmine and Nisha sees the five carat rock sitting on Shannon's hand they started screaming too. This commotion caused the waitress to come over, "Are you ladies ok?" she asks.

"Yeah we are." They apologized pointing to the ring that is causing the drama. When the waitress saw it she begins to scream like she knows them. She congratulates Shannon giving them free wine and desserts while they talk about how this happened.

Shannon told them all about John her sorry ass baby daddy. Leaving Jailah with Zane because he told him that he was her husband. The girls got a kick out

of the way Zane played John's punk ass.
It's time for Shannon to have a real man
come into her life. She isn't like her sister
Jasmine that got a great man on the first
try. She has one now Shannon isn't
letting go.

Nisha is happy for Shannon know
she going to be one of the bridesmaids.
Yet she is sad because she loves their
brother Staccz. She knows that she isn't
perfect but hell; who was?

"Nisha sis its gonna happen. Trust
me even if it's not with him; it will
happen." Jasmine says. Jay touches her
forehead to see if she is feverish. God

126

knows Nisha needs to hear that from the mouth she least expected it to come from.

"Thanks Jasmine that means so much coming from you." Nisha thanks her.

"Anytime." Jasmine is in a good mood thanks to her sister's news.

"Well since we all sharing news I just got my own place, Q is moving in with me." Jay shouts out. She is glad to tell someone.

"What really?" Shannon is shocked she starting to think working for Dallas was a great thing. It's making them all into woman.

The ladies talked and caught up on each other's lives. Everyone is doing well but talking to the ladies Nisha is ready to change the way she does things. She doesn't want to be left behind while all the others are growing and living life to the fullest.

She plans to change her way of living when she gets back from New York. First she has to go on this mission to make her mark so Dallas would know that she has a G code.

They were about to leave the place when Jay asks, "Jasmine didn't you meet up with Dallas yesterday?" Jasmine hoped no one asks.

"Yeah." was all Jasmine says.

"Well what's it about?" Shannon asks.

"Nothing just a run down on the plans for New York." She isn't a great liar all the woman knows it so they let it go heading home.

Dallas has taught the ladies a lot but obviously not enough. The whole time they were having a ball Cash was watching them. He is there with Venom enjoying a romantic dinner. That until Jay starts screaming about the ring that she caught his attention. There is no doubt in his mind that it was Jay.

He doesn't know the other women but he is sure they are her teammates. What is breaking his soul is that four woman broke his empire down to nothing. Stupid as it may seem he still loves Jay. She has Cash mind fucked up.

Venom notices the plus sized bitch that has her man's attention so much. She had to ask the nigga who the woman is. Cash doesn't lie when he stating *"My ex!"* The words cut Venom because she always thought he was here for more than he let on. Now the truth is coming out.

Chapter 14

This nigga Cash can't keep his eyes off Jay. He watched her until she was gone. Venom is so pissed that she left the place. She has never been disrespected like that ever in her fucking life. Now some South Cat clown is going to come use her for his own personal gain. Cash doesn't know it but he going to pay for making her feel like less than the queen she is; her family owns this fuck city.

Cash's mind is so fucked up. He knows that he is going to have to make shit up to Venom. She just doesn't understand what Jay has done to him.

That is his fault because he wasn't honest about why he was really here in the Lou.

Cash likes Venom but he hadn't open his heart up to love her. Due to the loss he had taken. Now that he seen Jay he knows why his heart couldn't love her. It was because he was in love with a woman that ripped his soul out. He feels like this woman has voodoo on him because he should be ready to kill her.

Yet all he wants to do is hug and tell her that he knows she was forced to do this. Cash just wants to be with her.

Duffle Bag Bitches 2

Venom is pissed to the tenth power she is in Cash's ride that he recently bought. Silently she is planning to dump his ass when he gets to her house. How the hell this sorry ass nigga gonna act like her and her sister don't own this fucking city! Venom jumps out of his ride slamming the door so fucking hard the window shatter. She never looks back at the sound of breaking glass.

"What the fuck man?" Cash follows her. He knows damn well why she was mad at him. If the shoe was on the other foot, he would have slapped the shit out of her.

"What the fuck? You really gonna ask me some dumb shit like that? Nigga do you know who the fuck I am? I got bitches and niggas in line to take your fucking spot. You gonna play me crazy over some lil fluffy bitch you used to fuck with?" Cash could have sworn he saw Venom's head spin.

"Baby I am sorry it's not like that. I didn't mean to hurt you. I am just shocked to see her here in the Lou. I almost married her. Hell she from SC so I'm wondering if she stalking me or some shit." He lies like a muthafucka.

Venom know he is lying too. That bitch's swag and tone reads STL all day. She doesn't know who the fuck he thinks he is fooling. "Almost married?" she asks.

"Yeah, I don't want to talk about her. Fuck her I am here with you baby." Cash barked.

"Oh you with me now that she is gone? Fuck you Cash." Venom is over him.

"Baby please don't do me like this. I can't take you doing me like this boo." Cash is down on his knees by this time.

Venom smiles because she knows what is going to come next. It was Cash's main copout when shit is heated. He kisses her navel and thighs as she moaned saying, "I am not giving you any pussy. So I hope that's not what you going for." Venom informs him.

"I know baby. J just let me taste it than I will leave." Cash begs.

Venom smiles because she knows that he isn't going to take no for answer. She didn't try to stop him. Cash continues to kiss and lick her inner thighs. He lifts her leg placing it on his shoulder. He loves the fact that Venom never wears panties when she has a dress.

Cash inserts his tongue into Venom's warm sweet pussy. She loves the way Cash feeds on her when he is in the wrong. It's a boost to her ego the way she makes him bow down.

"Oooohhhhhh argggggggh!" Venom is getting into it.

"Damn right mama rock that pussy on my face your nasty bitch." That shit drives Venom wild. She grabs the back of his head fucking his face as if this is the last face on the planet. Before Cash know it she hissing like a snake pulling away

138

from him, spraying her pussy venom all in his mouth as he sucks up every drop.

"Baby that pussy taste so good." Cash stands up licking his lips.

"I know now get the fuck out!" she opens the door to watch him walk out.

Cash takes the walk of shame to his car with his head hanging low. He feels real low right now. A part of him blames Jay for all of this. If only she would have just loved him.

Chapter 15

Beep beep beep...

The beeps are driving Mack crazy. He has been in a coma for a few months now. Its pissing him off that he can't get up and walk out of there. He lies there thinking

"I know some are wondering Mack are you mad at your team for leaving you behind? Truth is that in this life you have to know that it's live or die. If it was someone else that got hit they would have been left behind, including the women. In this life you do jail time for no one but yourself."

Mack is at peace with his team. He is glad Roc finally found them. He never gave information on the team whereabouts to anyone. Roc is his brother from his aunt that cared for him when his family passed.

Mack heard footsteps enter the room. He waits patiently to hear voices when he hears, *"This is not my nigga right here is it?"* Zane can't believe his eyes.

Dallas told Jasmine to tell no one but he has to tell Zane. Zane and Mack are the only family Dallas really has here in the Lou. He can't walk around knowing something like this, and not tell his brother. Zane would never forgive him if he left him in the dark like that.

The women are soft even when they appear to be strong. Dallas wants to spare them the heartbreak if Mack dies.

As a man he knows he had to let Zane know because it's only fair.

"Yeah man it's him." Dallas touches Zane's shoulder as he watches the tears fall from his eyes. Dallas has to look away from Zane or tears will appear in his own eyes.

"I knew these niggas loved a nigga like me. Always acting like they hard and

142

shit. Now his ass in here crying like a girl. I can't wait to I get up and tell his ass I heard him crying and shit." Mack thinks.

"How Dallas?" Zane asks.

Dallas explains to him about what went down between Shannon and Laura. That caused him to meet Roc. Roc brings him here; he even explains that Jasmine was the only person besides them that know that Mack is in this hospital or even still alive for that matter.

Mack is listening to everything they are talking about. He remembers Jasmine being there with Dallas and Roc a few days ago. The next thing he heard causes him to want to break out of the damn

coma.

"My wife loves this man. I think

almost as much as she loves me. If he

lives she couldn't ask for anything more

in the world I know it." Zane talking to

Dallas who is looking at him like he is

crazy.

"Your wife?" Dallas asks.

"That what the hell I am talking

about Dallas! When he get a damn wife? I

know not my sister Shannon." Mack

fusses as if someone could hear him.

144

"Shannon." Zane states thinking Dallas is slow or something. This makes Mack laugh.

"You married one of my girls without asking me?" Dallas says.

"Dallas must have forgotten who he was talking to." Mack thought.

"Ask you? That's funny! Who are you? Her father man? I don't need to ask you shit! I just told you she my wife." Zane looks back to Mack.

"That's my muthafuckin nigga Zane plays no games. He stands on what he believes." Mack thought smiling inward.

"Damn I am just saying I didn't get to come to the wedding or shit." Dallas fussing because his feelings are hurt.

"Look at his soft ass." Mack is still talking shit but no one knows it.

"Man I wouldn't do no shit like that; get married and leave you out. I would never do that; my wife wouldn't allow me to do that." Zane says to Dallas.

"She already got my nigga in a thong." If they could hear Mack Zane would fuck him up.

"Alright cool so when's the big day? I know we're going all out for this one."

Dallas is happy for his nigga and secretly hoping that he would finds a love one day.

"Yeah man we going to do it big. We're setting everything up after we get back from the New York mission." Zane is excited about his new life.

Mack thought about them doing another job. He fears that one of them could end up like him or worse. Before they even get to be married. The thought makes him sick to his stomach.

Zane looks at Mack feels a vibe come off him. That makes him think

Mack is trying to tell him something. He begins to talk to Mack like he is awoke.

"Man I'm glad that you still here with us. I-I didn't want to leave you I know that you wouldn't have wanted to leave me. I hope you can find it in your heart to forgive me. I haven't been able to find a way to forgive myself.

I wish you would wake up and be my best man. It would be the best wedding gift I could give to my wife. I thank you for schooling me on getting her. I almost let her crazy ass slip away. She's the best thing that ever happened to me bruh. I don't know what I would do if I lost her. So I guess I am saying I am willing to die for her or with her if the time comes. Ya dig? Man guess what I got a cute little step daughter? She looks like a black china doll.

I thought Shannon was a heart stealer but Jailah got her beat. Don't tell her I said that as a matter of fact tell her cause that means you came back to us. Man I hate sitting here talking about how good God has been to me. I know I don't deserve it for real. I got to go Mack because watching you like this is killing me trust I will be back." Zane walks out.

Dallas sees the tears flowing down Mack's cheeks he knows that Zane didn't see it. Mack heard every word that touched him causing him to say "Mack we love you bruh," as he exiting the room.

"I love y'all too." This time Mack spoke in a soft voice but no one is there to hear him.

Chapter 16

Jasmine know that she was going to catch hell. At the end of the week about the trip that she has to make. She is leaving Friday morning with Zane and Nisha. Jay, Shannon, and Dizzy will come the day before the mission takes place. Jasmine isn't in the mood to deal with what is coming her way. However, she doesn't have much of a choice.

The kids are still at school Korey hasn't left for work yet. He is in the living room playing the PlayStation 3. When Jasmine came in passing him a blunt. He looks at her because he has a sexy wife that he loves so much. Yet sometimes she seems to be more trouble than she's worth.

Jasmine looks at this gorgeous chocolate man. She often wonders why he bothers to stay with her all this time. She knows that she is a piece of work but some habits are die hard.

"What is it Jasmine?" Korey know it is something.

"You know I have to leave tomorrow?" She asks him.

"So?" He says as if he doesn't care but he does.

"What you mean so?" Jasmine asks him.

"What do you want me to say? Have a good trip, be safe because I won't?" He is honest about his feelings.

"I am doing this for us; for my family." Jasmine fussed.

"No you're not. You're doing this for yourself." By this time, Korey is on his feet.

"Where are you going?" Jasmine yells after him.

"To work because I do that for my family. Taking a chance on getting yourself killed is for money. It is not for your family. That's an ego trip you need to grow up! When you do I will be here waiting." Korey slams the door on his way out.

Jasmine sat on the couch bawling. She doesn't know how to make her husband understand what is going on. She thought about the offer Dallas made her. Korey is somewhat right; she loves the action and can't give up the life right now. Even if it was tearing her house or family apart.

For once in her life Jasmine feels like she is part of something. She loves her crew she hopes she never has to

choose between them or her husband.

Jasmine doesn't know who she would

choice.

Dizzy is coming out the police station talking to Detective Brown when Zane drives past heading home from the hospital. Most would have missed this action. Dallas school the no matter what always keep your eyes and ears to the street. In order to stay alive and free.

Zane has a funny feeling in his stomach for the second time today. Dizzy doesn't see Zane's car because he is talking and grinning from ear to ear. Zane has never seen this side of Dizzy. When he looked at Dizzy he is even dressed funny. Blazer, form fitting jeans, and a collared shirt with a tie, and square toed shoes. This nigga looks like a poindexter out this bitch.

Zane thinks the nigga have a court date as he continued to drive home. But something told him not to let this go. He decides to call Dizzy's phone to see if he will pick up.

The phone rings a few times then Dizzy picked picks up. "How may I help you?" That shit throws Zane off for a minute.

"Dizzy?" Zane asks knowing the nigga has his number locked in.

"Yes." Dizzy is tripping for real.

"Nigga this me Zane! What the fuck is up with you? Talking all proper and shit!" Zane is getting pissed that this nigga is trying to play games.

"I know who this is man. What's up? I am kind of in the middle of something right now." Dizzy's statement makes Zane feel even funnier.

Zane hears someone say "Good evening Detective Ross." He never heard Detective Ross respond. The name rings a bell to Zane because Ross is known for shutting down many major players in the game.

"Well man my bad I was just riding past the pig pen. You were out there wondering if you need a ride." Zane says lying about his call.

"I'm good! What you doing stalking me?" Dizzy asks sounding pissed.

"Not even player; just being a friend." Zane hangs up on the nigga before he gets pissed off.

The day that Zane having has to be what some consider a bad day. The feeling that he had in the hospital, at the police station when he sees Dizzy. Now Shannon is sitting on a park bench in front of his house.

159

Chapter 17

Shannon looks amazing as always in a gold glitter crew neck tee and Forsaken jeans from True Religion. Her shoe game is crazy she rocking the gold Giuseppe Zanottis. She is bad Zane loves everything about his woman. Nothing in this world has ever made him as happy. As she has in a few short months.

Shannon watches the gorgeous man exit his car wearing Michael Kors from head to toe. She often thinks designers made clothes just for him. The man is sexy in a major way. Shannon has been waiting on him for the past two hours never even bothering to call because she needed time to think about life.

Zane joined her on the bench kissing her on the cheek. "Hey beautiful what you doing out here? Spying on daddy?" Zane teases her.

"I am good babe." Shannon is very dry. The feeling in the pit of his stomach is getting worse after she spoke.

"What's the matter?" Zane asks even though he really doesn't want to know.

"I don't know." Shannon is lying he know it.

"Yes you do! Stop playing games; is it my little girl?" Zane I hoping that all is well with the little angel.

"She good babe." Shannon hates the way she feels.

"Come on Shannon speak now or forever hold your peace." Zane is getting pissed.

"I came by to tell you that we can't get married." Shannon says breaking his heart in to a million piece.

"What the fuck you mean?" Zane jumps off the bench. Zane begin pacing back and forth on the sidewalk.

"I don't want to get married. This is not for me; it will not last." Shannon is so confused that she doesn't know how to tell him the truth.

"Yes you do want to be married, this will last. I have never done this for any woman. I know this is real." Zane fussed.

"Look! I am not going to play games with this shit Zane. It's over." Shannon jumps off the bench walking away before he could see her tears falling. If he did he would never believe what she is saying.

Zane sat on the bench wondering what the hell is happening to his life. He couldn't believe that all this shit has transpired so fast. Mack is alive but not well enough to help him with this. Dizzy is all chummy with the police and shit. Now his wife to be doesn't want to be his wife anymore. He doesn't know why God is testing him. By placing the weight of the world on his shoulders. He doesn't know what to make of all this.

Shannon drives home thinking she doesn't like the way things went. She really loves Zane yet now is not the time to be in a relationship. Zane is a great man he is just what the doctor ordered for Shannon. Nevertheless, right now it is too much to deal with.

She knows that they are heading back to the field she already lost Mack out there. Shannon can't wrap her mind around what is taking place in her life. Shannon know if Zane gets hurt she would never be able to live with it.

Shannon know that it's unfair to walking away from the proposal like that. She looks down at her hand realizing that she still has the fucking ring on. Shannon is about to turn around so she could give it back. Yet her heart knows that there is no way she could walk away from Zane for the second time in one day.

Shannon really loves him she is afraid of losing him in this war they called life. If shit was different or the world was kind with money overflowing. She would hold on to him and never let go.

Zane is so broken behind what Shannon has done he doesn't know where to turn or who to run to. He thought about some of his old lady friends. Zane knows that even if he wastes his time on that. Once the nut is bust they would be no help to him.

He doesn't want to bother Dallas because he is getting things ready for them to move in a couple of days. He doesn't trust Dizzy anymore; something is off with dude. If what Zane feeling is right once he able prove it, he is going to kill him.

Zane called Jasmine to see if she could help. Her husband could at least do him this favor for letting him live. After he upping the burner on him.

"Hello Zane what do I owe the honor of this call to?" Jasmine hadn't gotten to know him like she should with him about to become her brother in laws.

"I need to talk to someone. I got so much crazy news today. If I don't share it with someone I am gonna lose it." Zane's voice sounds as if he is fighting to keep the tears from falling.

"I got to get my kids from school, find someone to sit with them. Then I can meet you bruh is that cool?" Jasmine wants him to know that she is there for him.

"Yeah I can be alone that long. Since you already know meet me at the hospital." Zane is going to talk to Mack even though he couldn't talk back.

"I will see you in a few hours. If you're not there I am coming to look for you." Jasmine loves her family she just has a hard way of showing it.

He laughs, "I am sure you will." Zane had never met their mother. He knows she has to be a good lady to raise her children to love the way they do.

Chapter 18

Dizzy walks into his house mad as hell slamming the door. Wondering how in the fuck he could be so careless to what the fuck is going on around him. He knows that he has to be mindful of Dallas's crew because they are all certified killers; especially the women.

Dizzy has to make the call to let his people know that he has been spotted at the precinct. "New York Police Department Sergeant Ricks speaking." Ricks speaks into the phone.

"Hey man what's up with you?" Dizzy asks.

Duffle Bag Bitches 2

"Man you better be calling me for a damn good reason. You know I don't really fuck with you like that Derrick." Ricks called Dizzy by his government name.

"Man fuck you! I am just calling you to let you know that I was spotted by one of the crew members." Dizzy schools his dumb ass.

"I knew that you would fuck this up! You can never do nothing right. You have been a fuck up since we were kids. Now we both joined this fucking pig squad trying to catch Dallas's ass all these years. Now he's heading to New York you about to blow our cover fucking up everything." Ricks is pissed with his baby bother.

Dizzy hates fact that he let his coward ass brother drag him into this bullshit. He is living good with the money Dallas is giving him. The reason that he is working as an undercover cop is because his brother Dawan Ricks used to run with Dallas back in the day in Portland.

Dawan got jammed up dimed Dallas out. Once Dallas got word that his boy put the people on him. The nigga skipped town been on the run ever since. Dizzy has always been a police officer. Dawan joined once he got out of the pen he found out that street life isn't for him.

Dizzy busted so many dope dealers in the past. He used to be shocked at the kind of life these niggas live. Yet here he is busting his ass to do what the fuck he thought is right barely making ends meet.

He was the good child out of him and his brother. Dizzy was on his way to becoming captain. That would have provided a great life for his wife and daughter.

Dizzy worked a case five years ago. A twenty-two-year-old boy that was worth a half a million at such a tender age was

his target. This was the biggest bust of

his career. Also a major turning point in

his life as well. The squad surrounded the

mansion that the young man lived in.

Chapter 19

The squad blew the door off the hinges filling the house to begin confiscating the money, weapons, and drugs. Dizzy is the one ordered to apprehend the young man. He really didn't want to be the one because some of these youngster is so wild that it was you or them.

Dizzy know that he has to follow the orders that were given to him in order to get the promotion. To Dizzy's surprise the young man is sitting behind a desk in a bedroom that he changed into an office.

He looks Dizzy in the eyes as if he is waiting for him to come.

The young boy puffs on a blunt that is full of sour diesel. The smell is amazing; Dizzy is an officer but he still smokes. The boy was at ease as Dizzy points his gun at him.

"I am going to need you to stand up and put your hands behind your back sir. Than come with me." Dizzy orders him. There was something about the young man and room that gave him an eerie feeling.

"Man how much they pay you to do this bullshit ass job?" the cocky young man asked.

"Man this is not the time to discuss money just do what I asked." Dizzy raises his voice.

"Not the time to talk money? That's why the fuck you here; to stop my hustle. So you can get a few more pennies in your pocket." The young man never raised his voice at all when he spoke.

"I make about forty thousand dollars a year." Dizzy tells him still holding the gun on him.

"Bahahahahahaha I make that a day." He puffs his blunt, "Hell if I was you I would be mad too." He removed a gun from his lap brought it into plain sight for Dizzy to see.

"Man don't do this my brother; it doesn't have to be this way." Dizzy don't want to shoot the kid.

"Be easy I am not gonna shoot you. This is a new beginning for you I understand but it's the end for me." The youngin cocked the gun.

"But it doesn't have to be!" Dizzy didn't know how to talk this kid out of this because his mind is made up.

178

"Yes it does!" The young man is over this life.

"Why?" Dizzy needs to keep him talking.

"Because I rule the world!" Then the kid blew his brains out.

The scene is fucked up but the other cops don't care because they still got what they were promised for the bust. Dizzy was promoted to captain as promised. He doesn't feel good about it but this is the job he chooses to do.

The shit got to him was that the cops handing over the guns and drugs but they pinch off the money. Most of them lived off drugs dealers; taking the money or being a part of their payroll. As the young men and woman rot in jail.

Dizzy still has an eerie feeling after the case was closed. He was sitting in his office when he got the call that he needs to get home as soon as possible. He rushes from the office not sure what is going. Something is telling him that shit is all fucked up.

When he arrived at his home he found it surrounded by police cars and ambulances. The sight causes his mind to think all kinds of shit but it doesn't prepare him for the shit his eyes sees when he enters the house. Dizzy's wife and five-year-old daughter are tied together in a chair. The baby was shot in the back and the same bullet that took her life took her mother's life by blowing her heart out.

Dizzy was confused about what the fuck took place in his house. He was a fucking cop; his family was supposed to be safe at all times. How the fuck could this happen to them he thought.

"Captain." one of the men called him.

Duffle Bag Bitches 2

Dizzy was fucked up as he walked over to the officer. He kept looking back at his wife and child wondering where he went wrong. The message that the officer showed him told him where he made his mistake, *"Because I rule the world!"* The words ate at his ass like acid.

The next thing Dizzy know the room started to spin everything went black.

When he woke he was in a mental hospital. They had committed him to when he wouldn't stop saying, "That bastard doesn't rule the fucking world." He kept repeating it so much they had to sedate him. Dizzy was in that place for six months. He had been demoted even though he worked his ass off on that case and lost his family.

They declared him mentally unstable then decided that he was no longer qualified for the captain position. When Dizzy was released from the hospital he never looked back at his job or home in Portland. He was on the first thing smoking to Saint Louis to start his life over if it's possible.

He got here bumped in to Dallas that was the day he decided to switch sides and walk on the wild side of life. He is living the good life he still getting over the fact that he lost his wife and child. Women are no issue to get but he can't bring his heart to love another. Dizzy know that when he called himself living the good life he wasn't able to keep his family safe. In this life he living now he is not about to chance that again.

The past six months has been hell on Dizzy. His brother Dawan Ricks found out he was working for Dallas. He begins talking about putting Dizzy away for life if he doesn't help bring Dallas down. The team is a bonus they could all walk away scott free as long as he has Dallas.

Dizzy told him that he would deliver but the truth of the matter is Dizzy likes his life. He isn't ready to give it up just to please his bitch ass brother. Yet he has to play the game for what it is right now to buy himself time.

Chapter 20

Mack know that Zane was in the room with him but he doesn't know why cause the nigga isn't talking to him. Mack is so tired of being awake and no one knowing because his stupid ass body is still in a coma. He is fussing at his legs because he has been trying to will them to move.

They say that the body is controlled by the brain. That shit doesn't seem to be working for him. Mack's thoughts are broken by the sounds of heels entering his room. He knows damn well it isn't a damn nurse because they been able to wear heels he would have been awake by now. The voice that follows the sound of the heels changed his mind frame.

"Hey Zane." Jasmine spoke when she came in the room. Mack thought, *"That's just Jasmine's stinking ass."* She kissed him on the cheek feels good to him because he hasn't touched a woman in months. The way she made him feel makes Mack mad so he fussed some more in his head *"Don't be fucking kissing on me and shit girl. I been and put something off in you."* He is crazy and he doesn't know about her crazy husband.

"Hey sis I didn't think you was going to make it." Zane had been there about two hours just sitting with his boy and thinking.

"Yeah it took me a minute to get someone to sit with those bad kids of mine." Jasmine jokes trying to bring some joy to the room. Mack in a coma, Zane down, and fighting with her husband she thanks God for her kids cause right now they are the only people making her smile.

"It's cool sis I just needed someone to talk to about this shit Shannon just pulled on me for no reason at all." Zane begins to talk fast and pace the room.

Mack thought, *"Here this bitch ass nigga goes whining about some shit." He hates that about Zane; he was a great looking man but easily discouraged.*

Jasmine doesn't know shit about Shannon and him not being on good terms. The last time she seen her sister she was flashing a rock and a smile.

"What are you talking about Zane?" Jasmine has to ask because she is lost.

"She called the damn wedding off for no fucking reason. She just showed up at my house on this bullshit." Zane is pissed at her doing this.

Mack can't believe his ears that she had called it off so soon. Than he thought about himself laying in this bed or the fact that the whole team had to leave him for dead. Shannon could never do that to her husband so he understands her feelings. That was part of the reason he never had a real woman.

"I'm sorry, she didn't tell me anything about that. The last time I saw her she was showing me a huge ring. Shannon was happy about the new life you all were about to live. She just has

cold feet baby that's all." Jasmine
assured him. She can't wait to talk to
Shannon and cuss her ass out.

"Cold feet for what Jasmine?" Zane
is in love he forgot that his life is far from
normal. He never even thought about
losing her in this war they lived in called
life.

Mack knows this nigga has to be
smoking. *"Fool you work for Dallas; you
can die, go to jail, or be laying in this bed
like me."* Mack know that no one could
hear him but it doesn't stop him from
talking.

191

"It's the life we all have chosen to live. Shannon is scared of losing you. She didn't say that because she knows that you would assure her that nothing would happen to you. She made the decision for you by calling the wedding off." Jasmine schools him.

"I can promise her that nothing will ever tear us apart." Zane knows that is a lie but what else is he to do. Life without Shannon he is pointless.

"No you can't; that why my husband is so mad at me now. No matter how much money I bring home. I will never be able to promise him or my four children that as long as I live this life." Jasmine confesses. She knows Korey is right she just isn't about to quit now. She is close to having them set for life she just prays daily that she fore fills that promise.

"Well what do I do sis just let her go?" Zane know that he couldn't do that.

"No! I don't know yet. Let me talk to her see how serious she is about this. If know my sister she's hurting right now. Only you will be able to mend her heart." Jasmine know that Shannon loves Zane very much so she would see what she could to do in his favor. After all her husband did try to kill him.

193

"Thanks Sis I need all the help I can get on this one." Zane told her.

"Look at his cry baby ass nigga bitching up. If Shannon was my damn woman I would tell her, we getting married and that's it." Mack thought.

"I got you boo no worries." Jasmine looks at her watch knowing it's time for her to be heading back home. She kisses Mack heading out the door.

Zane doesn't have anywhere to be so he stays with Mack. Sometime after Jasmine left Zane ends up dosing off for an hour or so. For a minute he forgot where he is until he looks over at the bed that housed his homie. All these tubes running in and out of him. Zane hates to see Mack this way but he isn't going to give up on him. This his brother no matter what.

He wished the nigga would get up and say something. Zane has to laugh at his own thoughts because he knows once Mack is up and talking shit. He would be ready to knock that nigga back into a coma. That is the crazy part because Zane can't wait to have that feeling again. He needs Mack's shit talking ass in his life.

Chapter 21

Mack could feel Zane stirring; that is one of the qualities he had developed since he has been in the coma. He can feel people movements way before they ever spoke. Mack is tired of being in this coma even though his family came to visit the visits are coming less and less.

Now that Dallas and Zane have been visiting him he hasn't see Roc much but he knows that nigga is tired. He has been with Mack daily since this took place. Even when Roc's woman would complain he didn't care what she said. He was gonna be there for Mack.

Dallas and Zane being around helps Roc out a lot. Mack appreciates all the time they put in but it's time to get out this bed or die. He is not willing to be on this earth in this state any longer. Zane has been there all day and Jasmine has come and left.

Mack know that Zane will be heading out soon. He will be stuck here in this damn hospital bed listening to the beeps from these stupid ass machines.

Zane begin to stretch and stand up. He looks at his Rolex that read midnight. He knows that he has been there too long. It's time for him to head home to get

197

some rest. Tomorrow he has the team meeting with Dallas then it's off to New York for him.

He is glad that he has spent the time with Mack. The life Zane lives you are not always promised to make it back. When people choose this lifestyle they have to think long and hard because you are risking your life and freedom for the money every day.

Zane walks up to Mack's bedside to bid him goodnight. Mack know that Zane would always grab ahold of his hand before he left. He never kissed him like Jasmine. Mack is grateful for the kiss

198

gets a women's touch of sensitivity every now and then. That is good for him. Men are cool to visit but sometimes you need feminine love to make it through the day.

Zane begin to talk to Mack, "Aye man I am gonna have to get up on out of here. I got a meeting with Dallas in the am. I need to get to my bed and get a little shut eye."

Mack let a single tear slide down his cheek because he is sick of laying in that bed. Alone at night having no life at all.

Zane continued to talk, "When I get back from this mission. This is the first place I am coming. You hear me my dude?" Zane got quite like he is waiting for Mack to speak but he didn't.

Zane know that is his cue that it is time to shake. He grabs Mack's hand as he always did before leaving. As he tries to let go he couldn't. At first Zane thought he was tripping or tired.

He pulls his hand away again but Mack holds on; he isn't about to let Zane walk out of the room today. He is ready to get out of that damn bed.

Zane began yelling at him "Nigga you woke?" Zane is tripping.

"Say something bruh!" He barked another order forgetting the man had been in a coma for months. Still has tubes running down his throat.

"Mack if you woke and can hear me squeeze my hand." Zane told him.

Mack took all the power he had to squeeze Zane's hand. His body had been stiff for so long that it caused a little pain trying to squeeze Zane's hand but he manages to do it.

Zane was geeked up he wide awake after that. He ran out into the hallway yelling, "He's awake! My nigga woke up!" The nurse thinks Zane has lost his mind sitting in that room all day. Now here he

is in their hallway yelling and carrying

on.

She walks over to him and asked,

"Sir are you ok?" She tries to stay

professional because no matter how crazy

Zane looks at the moment he was still

fine as a muthafucka.

"Yeah I am great baby! It's my homie

in 303. He's been in a coma for minute he

woke now." Zane picked her up kissing

her on the cheek, "He awake boo!" He is

too damn happy.

"Sir calm down we can go take a

look at him." She has to calm herself

because this nigga picking her up had caused her panties to get wet.

The nurse heads to the room. She knows that Zane is following close by because she can smell his cologne. She enters the room walking over to the bed. She could tell that something is happening with Mack because his heart rate has increased.

She began to speak to him even though she knows that he couldn't respond due to the tubes. "Mr. Walker are you coherent now?" Mack is thinking, *"Bitch I don't know what you talking about but I know that I can hear."*

She came to her senses she removed the covers from his feet "Wiggle your toes if you can hear me." She orders Mack.

He moved his toes without any trouble at all. She knows than that Zane is right Mack is responding. Before she could say anything Zane chimes, "I told you he woke.

"Yes he did, let me get the doctor." She rushes from the room.

Zane continued to talk to Mack as the nurse went to find the doctor. "Man I can't believe that you are really awake. This is the day I have been sitting here waiting for." Mack know that Zane was excited about him coming out the coma.

Mack eyes began to flutter as he is trying to open them so that he could show Zane that he is really was awake. Zane watched his homie open his eyes it made a smile come across his face to knowing that his boy was back.

It took everything in Zane to keep his tears from falling. He a softy at heart but the gangsta in him keeps the tears in check. Mack know his partner all too well. He knew Zane was ready to bawl like a bitch. The thought the love behind the emotions means something special to

Mack. He has a whole lot of people that care about him.

Chapter 22

The nurse reenters the room with the doctor and a few other staff members following. The doctor begins to examine Mack to see what kind of condition his mind and body are in. The doctor us very shocked to find all of his levels normal. Most people that come out of a coma are really irate this man seems to be cool as a cucumber.

"He's very much out of the coma all his vitals are normal." The doctor informs Zane.

"That's great Doc! I'm so glad to hear that. This is the moment me and my family have been waiting for." After Zane make the statement when he realizes that he had never contact Dallas or Roc with the great news.

"Well sir I am glad that you were here to witness your friend's recovery. We will begin removing the tube in his throat. It will be hard for him to talk but he will be able to whisper. You will have to listen to him closely." The doctor schools him on what will be taking place.

"That's great Doc. I understand that he will have to take things one day at a time. Once we get him home." Zane is ready to pack that fool up right then.

"Slow down Sir; he is awake but he won't be leaving here for a few more weeks. Even so after that he will still have limitations requiring home physical therapy." Mack is pissed listening to the fact that he would have to stay for a few more weeks.

That is bullshit to him but he knows that he would have to get some help to get this stiff ass body back in working order.

"I understand Sir. Now is it okay to call my family?" Zane asks.

"Sure thing son, go right ahead you gangsters have such love for each other."

209

Mack wants to slap the shit out of his white ass. Well the nigga is black but acts like a white man.

Zane ole Good Samaritan ass is saying, "Yeah we do!" Then he steps outside the room as the techs went to work on Mack.

Zane couldn't wait to tell Dallas. He isn't worried about him answering the phone. Zane know that Dallas would pick up on the first ring due to the time of night it is. Dallas is always on top of late night calls because his hoes or hustlers could be hurt. He wants to know the minute it happened. Dallas is sleeping he fumbles with the phone. "State your business than get off my phone." Dallas has a way with words.

"He woke my nigga." Zane's happy ass chimes.

"Who?" Dallas know Zane's voice but for a minute he forgot that Mack is in a coma or even alive.

"Mack nigga! What the fuck is wrong with you? Let me find out you got some bad bitch over there sucking your brains out." Zane is a fool Dallas had to laugh at his crazy ass.

Duffle Bag Bitches 2

"Naw bruh, I am not on any shit like that. You got to be bullshitting me that my nigga woke. Look G I am on my muthafuckin way. Don't you move family." Dallas hops out of bed into some sweatpants and a fresh T-shirt to go greet his homie. He wishes he could bring the nigga some champagne but he knows it is way too soon for that.

Shannon gazes out the window wondering how Friday got there so fast. It is only five in the morning but lately she has been having a hard time sleeping. Zane is heavy on her mind. She looks over at her sleeping daughter. She loves that little girl more than anything. That was the only reason she risking her life.

Shannon looks back out the window thinking about Zane. Wondering if he misses her as much as she misses him. Even though she is the one who called everything off. She knows that it would be hard to face him today at the meeting. Shannon really do love him.

Once she thought about how she loss Mack there is no way she is going on this New York trip as a couple. If she he gets killed everything in her would die. Little does she know that wife or not. If Zane gets hurt her mind will not be able to handle it. A part of her will die as well.

Shannon hopes that he doesn't think she is selfish for playing with his heart. She caused him to open up then just leaving hanging. She has never love anyone but her daughter's father. That is nothing compared to the way she loves Zane. Shannon never meant to hurt

Zane. She really wants what is best for him when it's all said and done.

She has to put the idea in her head to get herself out of this now. Before there is no turning back. Even though she can't turn off the love she has for him no matter how hard she tried. As she walks away from the window to get a move on her day. Shannon looks at her hand that still carries the rock that he gave her.

Shannon know that it's time to take it off and move on with her life. She isn't willing to take a chance with her heart again. Shannon has hardened her heart.

She can't allow Zane to break her heart all over again.

"Anyway he doesn't need a woman like me," Shannon tells herself, *"I am damaged and broken. What good could I be bringing that kind of a baggage into his life."* She hopes in the shower hoping that her pain, hurt, and shame will wash down the drain with dirt and love she has for Zane.

Chapter 23

Nisha is ready for the trip as she lies in bed in hot pink *Dream Angels* lace-trimmed satin slip by Victoria Secret. She is ready to make a name for herself this time around. She feels that she let Dallas down by breaking rules. That he placed for their safety.

"If I had listened." She keeps telling herself. Every time she faces Dallas she feels that she needs to prove herself to him. She has done it once with the nigga West. She can do it again.

Nisha has seen so much in this new life. Yet, most of all she wants what

217

Shannon has with Zane. She wishes their brother would get it together. Become the man that her family needs him to be. He continues to fuck up.

Nisha doesn't know who to blame anymore. Staccz for doing the dumb shit he does or herself for staying around putting up with it. She is sick and tired of the lies, tearful nights, and empty promises that he always makes her believe.

Nisha know that he will never change until she changes her mind set on life. Showing him that she is a woman with or without him. Most women don't know that when you put too much faith in a man. He will know that he can yo-yo you until the string breaks.

Nisha is used to being babied by her mother. Who took care of the kids for her. As she prances around like she is a Barbie doll. Today she wants more out of life but it all would have to wait until she gets back from this trip.

This is her chance to show her team that she is ride or die for them. She knows they all questions her due to her childish ways and the way she lives.

Once she returns home she plans to do something with her life. Nisha hopes her baby daddy is ready to get his shit together. If not, he is going to see her love someone else. She has already waste enough time on loving him. At this point of life, she is going to love Nisha.

Nisha has also heard rumors that Nick B is on to her ass. He plans to catch her when she least expects it. She plans to talk to Dallas about making that little troublemaker go away. Nisha know that she is the cause of his brother losing his life.

However, she doesn't plan to pay Nick B back with her blood. So Nisha has to send him to his resting place as well.

"Nick B doesn't know who he fucking with

I'm a Duffle Bag Bitch!" she thinks to

herself. Little does she know Nick B isn't

to be fucked with either.

Jasmine made love to her husband before breaking that bad news to him. That she was leaving Saturday morning. Korey isn't wild with his wife's new job. The morning they shared was so great, and long overdue.

Korey silently prays that she will be safe because he can't imagine life without her. He isn't in the mood to argue over things he can't change. That is who he married; a woman that wants things her way or no way at all.

Once her mind is made up no matter if she is right or wrong. Jasmine isn't going to give in.

Jasmine often thinks about the offer that Dallas gave her. Its sweet of him to let her out of the crew. Yet something will not allow her to walk away. For the first time she is a part of something much bigger than herself.

She doesn't want to lose that feeling. Jasmine know that she is selfish risking her life. Knowing that she has a husband and four children.

Deep down inside she knows that she made a life for herself too fast. Once you make a bed you have to lie in it. Jasmine put on her big girl panties taking care of the family she made. She is going find a way to keep the new found excitement. That had been missing in her life.

At this moment lying in her husband's arms feels good. It scares her to think that there is a possibility this could be her last time laying with her love.

Jay has been spending so much time with Q. She doesn't know whether she is coming or going. Jay loving every minute of it. She has a new place and man life is great. Jay is wondering where her life with Q is going. She is on that

Deborah Cox shit, *"Nobody supposed to be here."*

Things are grand from where she is standing or so she thinks. Little does she know Cash has been watching her ever move. He can never get his hands on her.

Thanks to her new found man/guardian angel that is always with her when she moves around. She is beginning to love all the love Q is showing her. Yet it scares her a little bit too. Jay like most women she has been fucked over more than a time or two.

That's how you learn to be careful who you give your heart to. She can see that Q is different from all the other man she had in the past. He takes her places, buy her gifts, and wants all her time. loves the way this man is treating her. Yet she watches very closely for any changes.

Jay hasn't notice the week has gone by so fast. Her and Q has been out partying, dinners, movies, shopping, long walks in the park, etc.... Jay wishes she could put him in her suitcase take him with her.

The whining he done once she told him she is leaving doesn't make it much better. Jay know that she is going to miss the passionate love they been making all week.

Duty calls Dallas doesn't play about money. It's time to pick the number on this New York clown. His stunting days are coming to an end. Jay rolls over in bed kissing. Q Then exits the bed in her birthday suit. Q watches her; he hates to see her go yet love to see her walk away.

This woman has stolen his heart in a short time in return she gave him hers. Q isn't the kind of man that fall easily or jocks women like he has Jay. Q is what you call a player until Jay came laying hands on him.

That is moment he turned his player card in ready to become a fully committed man.

Chapter 24

The meeting with Dallas is set for noon. Those departing today will be leaving around five pm. The girls are in route Dizzy thinks to himself. As he heads to the meeting. He was ordered to call all the women make sure they are getting a move on.

He knows that women often take too damn long to get ready. The thought makes Dizzy laugh because he thinks about how he would rush his wife along. When they had important dinner dates. He truly misses his wife and daughter. It is funny how so many years can pass you by. Yet the hurt is still the same as the day you found out.

Dizzy has thought of moving on many of times but his heart just wouldn't let go of the painful past. That he often tries to put behind him. He watches Zane with Shannon. The sight made him want to love again. Yet the scars he has never seem to mend.

Then he shakes the thought away from his mind or more so the tears. That are trying to fall from his eyes. It is still strange to him because it is usually Zane's job round up all the ladies.

Lately Dizzy's wife has been coming to him in his dreams. Telling him that it was time to take his life back. He knows what she meant he just doesn't know if he has the strength to pull it off. If he even cares enough to give life a second chance.

Dizzy's brother Lt. Ricks has been blowing his phone up so much he feels like he has a main bitch to check in with. The shit with his brother is getting out of hand. After this New York trip he plans to end this shit with him once and for all.

Fuck the police is all he could think. They just threw him away after his family was killed behind one of their drug busts. This was how they repaid him. Now his coward ass brother blackmailing him into some shit that he doesn't want to be a part of.

This beef Ricks has with Dallas is not just police business. Dizzy is going to prove it before he fucks around and get himself killed.

Zane has been spending day in and day out at the hospital with Mack. In a short amount of time that nigga has been talking Zane is ready to knock his ass back in a coma.

More than anything he is glad that his boy has coming back to his life right before his eyes. Zane stays at the hospital waiting for Dallas and Roc to show their faces. Once they did get there that nigga Mack was sitting up in bed eating ice and Jell-O that the doctor okayed him to have.

The two men are shocked to see the nigga back moving again. Mack couldn't say much because his throat is still sore but he eyes Roc to say thank you for saving my life. I will be forever grateful for that. The same eyes told Dallas I understand this is the game we play. No offense taken for leaving me behind.

Both men heard the word that Mack's eyes spoke. Roc holds a sense of pride for what he has done. Dallas holds regret he swore to never let another man on his team be left for dead. He plans to speak to Roc to see how soon his crew could join the Duffle Bag Crew.

Zane stayed at the hospital till 2 am. He knows that he needs a few hours of shut eye.

Zane is dying inside about the shit that is going on with him and Shannon. He missing the hell out of her, Zane needs her in his life. He doesn't bother trying to call. Just drove past the house a few times.

Zane hates the times when he rode past seeing her and Jailah out playing in the front of her building or getting in the car to go somewhere. He doesn't understand how she could let him go so easily. Because he knows the love they share is strong and more than worth holding on to.

Somehow something willed Shannon to let go, all the while he is still holding on. At first he thought maybe she never loved him, it was just a little fling. Then his heart would protest this is the real thing. Zane doesn't understand what is standing in the way of his fairytale love story.

Shit is wild there is nothing he can do to fix the pain. Zane feels in his heart at this moment. Hopefully the killing that he will be doing in a few days will ease some of the hurt. Zane has gone home to rest, yet it is slow to come. Once he finally closes his eyes at 3 a.m. he finds them open wide awake again at seven am.

The apartment doesn't feel the same anymore. He is almost ready to move to get rid of the memories of time him and Shannon spent there. Now he understands why he never brought women to his home.

As he laid there he has nothing else to do. The meeting is more than six hours away. Zane showers heads back to the hospital with Mack. He is sure that his boy could use the company; God knows he could.

Zane wrapped with Mack for about an hour before they took him off to therapy. He told him about what has taken place with him and Shannon. Mack is happy for him at the same he hates to see the pain that Shannon causing his dude.

Mack also found out that Jasmine is the only one out the women who know that he was in a coma. None of them know that he is awake. He asked Dallas to keep it on the hush because he doesn't want to see any of them until he is back up to full speed.

Physical therapy is a bitch Mack is feeling the pain as the therapist helps him walk back to his room. He never would have imagined that something so easy as walking could be so painful. As he enters the room he thinks the emotional pain that he is watching his friend go through us a lot worse. That caused him to be thankful for his physical pain. Emotional pain hurts beyond your wildest dreams.

Chapter 25

Zane is sitting in the same spot he was sitting when Mack left the room two hours ago. He is feeling sorry for himself when Mack gets back in bed from rehab.

The nurse helps him back to the bed he looks at Zane. Mack wondering why this nigga letting his troubles win lately. That is not Zane's style; he a fighter, the kind of nigga that bounces back easily. Something is way off this time.

The only thing that Mack could think of is that Shannon is really the one. You know how it is when you find and lose it. Nothing will ever be the same until you get it back.

Zane is just sitting there staring at his phone. Mack is sick of the shit already. If Shannon doesn't think he is dead, he would have called her himself. Hell he has half a mind to call her ass scare the hell out of her. By telling her if she doesn't take Zane back he will haunt her for the rest of her life.

Mack grabs the phone out of his hand, "What the hell you texting Shannon?" Mack tries to make light of the issues at hand.

"Man give me my damn phone."

Zane grabs it back but it is too late. Mack

sees the picture of her he is looking at.

He knows for sure that the nigga is a love

sick puppy.

"Nigga is the pussy that good? That

you have to stare at her pictures? I know

y'all broke up and shit. Damn I am

jealous, I got to find me a bad bitch like

that!" Mack teased him still trying to ease

the man's hurt.

"Yeah it is that good I'm staring at

the picture because I haven't seen her in

a while." Zane has to laugh at the answer

he gave but he is still sad. Mack could see it all over his face he hates it.

"What the hell you going to do about it?" Mack feels fuck it do whatever it takes to fix it. If you this lost without her.

The statement make Zane hurt even more "She called the wedding off the day you woke up. That's why me and Jasmine were here. I needed to talk to her to see if I could find some answers. She is no help either. Jasmine is a great sis and listener fosho though." He hates that shit is all fucked up.

"So what you gonna do?" Mack asks him again now that he has more facts.

"About what?" Zane is irritated.

"Getting your muthafuckin woman back?" Mack is getting mad because this nigga was acting like a bitch. This is not like Zane.

"There's nothing to do. She called it off, even told me she doesn't want to get married to me." Zane jumps out of his chair begin to pace the floor. He is pissed because he came here to take his mind off her yet it is no use.

The sight of him is making Mack sick "Yes the fuck there is something to fight for! The women she said she don't want to get married. She didn't say she don't love you." Mack yells at his stupid ass.

Zane doesn't know what to say because she never said that, "No she didn't." he finally says thinking back on the day she called it off.

"Well then it's not that she doesn't want to marry you. She's running from something your bitch ass is in here staring at pictures letting her get away." Mack fusses. He is glad to be back because he is much needed.

"You're right my nigga. I will find a way to make her take me back." Zane looks at his watch than said, "Now it's time to head to New York to get this money." Zane is glad that his boy is alive and able to give him the push he needs from time to time.

Life is good he doesn't know exactly what he would do but he plans to make his homie proud of him.

Zane walks out the door heading to Dallas's house for the meeting. Mack watches the boy. Now understands why God sent him back to this ratchet ass world. He is glad to be here. A part of him wishes that he was going with the crew to New York.

He know that is a crazy thought since he just got his life back. The crew is all he know they hav always taken care of him; even now. It is a life he wouldn't trade for anything in the world. Mack plans to live and die for his crew.

Mack yells, "Your welcome" knowing that Zane is long gone. It feel good to know that even from that bed he could be a helping hand when needed. Mack is labeled a fool yet is a very wise man that often used humor to get through life.

If he doesn't there would be no need for bullets because life alone would have killed him. He has built a laughter barrier that make him look strong even when he

weak. This very moment as he thinks to

himself, how blessed he is blessed.

Chapter 26

Dallas is waiting to start the meeting when Zane walks in. Dallas has so much shit that he has put in motion in just the few hours that Mack has been awake. That he is still in the clothing he wore to the hospital.

Zane has run home to change. He has been a slob for the past few days. He know that he would never get Shannon back that way. She is too strong to feel sorry for a bum ass nigga.

Zane jump clean on her ass. He has on a dark brown and orange Gucci jacquard piqué cotton with

249

green/red/green signature web detail. Dark brown interlocking G patch jogging pants.

Beige/ebony GG plus with cured colored leather and crocodile trim shoes. Woven leather necklace with the Gucci crest and grey/white/brick Havana plastic shades while smelling like Gucci Guilty fresh from the Gucci store.

That nigga is so muthafuckin clean that Shannon lowers her head when he walks in.

All four women are looking as flawless as ever. These bitches live in the mall loves to stay pressed. That is one of the things that Dallas admires about all of them. They take pride in their looks.

Dizzy even looking fly but none of them could touch Zane today. He is turned up he know that the crew know it. When Dallas calls him out, "Well glad you could join us small people Mr. Money Bags." He teases Zane thinking, *"I am going to have to go shopping with that nigga next time."*

"What man? This old shit? It's nothing." Zane sits down in a chair next to Shannon. He looks at her as he removes his shades, "Hey girl." Zane's mouth saysbut his ocean blue eyes and

Gucci cologne has stolen Shannon's heart again.

She doesn't even know that she is speechless until Jasmine pushes her, "He said Hi sister." Jasmine is laughing at Shannon's dumb ass.

"I heard him bitch!" She hates Jasmine at times because she always the one to point some shit out.

"Hey love!" she says then crossed her legs because she is soaking wet Zane know it. When she asks "Dallas can we get a move on with this meeting so I can go?" Dallas laughed because he know women like the back of his hand. Shannon is ready to fuck.

"Sure thing Ms. Shot Caller." He gave Zane a wink.

Zane nods his head saying, "You the man." He looks at Shannon. He loving to watch her sweat. Zane wants to end the act kiss her. He has to keep it up until he know that she will be his wife.

"Well damn everybody got special names can I get one?" Jasmine fusses.

"Yes you can Ms. Loud Ass." Dallas shut her ass up real fast.

Duffle Bag Bitches 2

Dallas walks around the room looking over everyone. He know the movement of everyone that works for him. Even when they think he isn't watching. He even knows about the police working for him. Dizzy doesn't know that he is on to him because Dallas never acts as if he knows anything until he has all the facts. Now is not the time to expose him. He was going to tell them about Mack. However, Mack asks him not to just yet. He respected that.

"Well we all know Shannon killed Laura here a few weeks ago right?" The crew is shocked because no one know but Jay.

"When?" Jasmine asks.

"Why? Dizzy questioned.

"How?" Nisha is clueless.

"Who gave the order?" Zane wants to know why she is killing hookers. He know it wasn't over that little beef they had.

Dallas shakes his head at all the questions, "Shannon would you like to answer your family?" he asks.

"It was last month Jasmine." She rolls her eyes at her nosy ass sister.

"Dizzy she lied on me. So I put her ass to rest." Dizzy stares at her in a state of shock.

"Nisha I blew her fucking brains out." That scares Nisha.

"Zane, Dallas was about to let the bitch walk away from the family. We all know this crew is until death do us part. So I gave her a pardon." She smiles at him with a sexy smile. That makes his dick hard causing him to shift in his seat.

Jay shakes her head at the crazy ass girl. Jasmine is pissed that Shannon didn't tell her big sister about this.

"Muthafuckas sure be keeping shit hidden." Dallas shakes his head at Jasmine.

Nisha became scared of Shannon isn't sure if she trusts her anymore. Dizzy wishes he had her powers that way he could get rid of his sorry ass brother.

Shannon has turned the tables Zane is in love all over again. Dallas laughs at the looks on his teams faces behind this woman's words.

"Now that we got that out the way. I want to let everyone know that the headquarters will be moved to a new location. By the time you make it back from New York next week. You will be informed on the new location when you touch back down in the Lou. This warehouse has become too hot."

"I have also sold my house that sits in the back of this place. I will no longer have my home in the same location as the warehouse. My home location will be on a need to know basis. It's funny now days you just never know who you can trust. Right Dizzy?" Dallas asks trying to put the nigga in the hot seat.

"You're so right about that my nigga." The statement makes Zane laugh at the pig.

Dizzy shot him a look that is not friendly. He is pissed that his brother has his crew second guessing him on the low. The thought of it made him sick to his stomach causing him to sweat.

Chapter 27

Jasmine came to his defense "Well we don't have to worry about that. In this family isn't that right Dizzy?" She asks.

"Damn right sis! None of that over here." He could stand his ground with someone on his side. Even if he is lying thought his teeth.

"Glad to hear that my nigga." Dallas rolls his eye like a bitch at Jasmine. She is always putting in her two cents when no one has asks to borrow the shit.

"Okay we in and out of New York in four days. No bullshit last time we were sloppy because one of our men got hit. That's not gonna happen this time. Pretty boy Floyd over there." Dallas points to Zane, "Already has a semi-friendship established with Eric. The nigga an undercover fag and major stunner. That's holding crazy paper we want it."

"He's not using the money the right way anyway. So let's ease in and out. I meant what I said about no fuck ups. Zane, Nisha, and Jay you'll head to the airport when you leave here. Shannon, Jasmine, and Dizzy y'all fly in on day three." Dallas ends the meeting on that note.

Zane is getting ready to walk out of the room. When Shannon grabs his hand, "It is nice to see you." She smiles. He was about to respond when his phone rings.

"Hello." He picks up while still holding her hand. This is just what he needs to drive her wild.

"What girl? I am on my way out of town." Zane says into the phone while Shannon watches him she gets pissed.

"Look baby don't act like that. I will get with you when I get back." Zane stands there fussing.

"Hold on girl," he looks at Shannon.

"Yeah likewise its good seeing you too."

He put the phone back to his ear walking

out the door talking to the woman.

Shannon so mad she could have spit

bullets.

Dallas watches it all he know what

Zane is doing and why. He is loving every

minute of the shit. It is about time that

nigga showed Shannon that he is going to

live and be happy with or without.

Sometime people need to know that to

learn the value you bring to their life.

Dizzy and Jasmine are chatting in

the corner together having a long talk.

Dallas wonders what the two of them are huddled so close together talking about. He is hoping like hell that Jasmine doesn't have anything to do with Dizzy being the police.

If she does her husband will really be looking for him cause the both of them dead. Dallas hates to even think that way about his crew. He still has plans to keep a close eye on it all. Dallas plans to hang around the hospital with Mack while the workers he hired move all the things from the old warehouse to the new warehouse.

The new warehouse will not only have a full recreation room. That is equipped with television, video game system, stereo system, pool tables, and a bar. Dallas has done his thing in the new warehouse. That is not all it offers. It also have a mini hospital and rehabilitation center for crew members that get injured in the field.

Now they will be saved if God agrees thanks to the new addition to the crew. The Duffle Bag Rescue team.

He doesn't bother to tell the team about them because they were going to be an undercover unit. Only seen as needed. Their job is to get the fallen crew member back to safety. Dallas likes the idea that he and Roc came up with.

Everyone know that is the name of the game. If you are shot or worse you're left behind for dead or jail. That is the reason niggas that lived after taking a shot to the head ratted their whole crew out. No one really wants to be left to die alone and cold.

Roc is the head of it all. He has a team made up of Tim, Bunz, and J-Roc. They already work for him that's how he saved Mack's life. Come to find out that Roc and his crew has been watching Mack's back for years. For a minute

Dallas was pissed to think that strangers know how his crew moved.

That is not good for business because that gives a nigga a chance to sell your ass up the river. But hell look how they did for Mack. It is most definitely time for a change.

Dallas is so glad to have them. He know the members they all checked out. A nice long line of history in crime no disloyalty is heard when you speak their names in the street. That makes Dallas comfortable welcoming them aboard.

He doesn't want to bury anyone on his team. Unless they wrong him or the crew. That someone wronging his crew makes him think of Dizzy. He can't believe it the boy is a stone cold killer like that working for the police. Dallas has never questioned who Dizzy was because he just started out when joining his team.

Shortly after the South Carolina trip it was the little shit that people peeping. Dizzy has always been distant that is his choice. As long as he is down when it is time to put in work.

Chapter 28

Dizzy has put down more niggas than his whole crew. The police is the muthafucka doing all the killing this shit crazy. The shit makes no sense to him. Once he done some digging Dallas found out about the shit that happened to his family.

The shit is fucked up unbelievable that they would play the nigga so cold. After all the work he done for their ass. Dallas know police or not the man is boarder line insane.

Due to shit that he has been through over the past few years. Dallas also found out that Ricks is Dizzy's brother. He know why Ricks is after him so bad.

When Ricks got jammed up Dallas was supposed to be there that night too. Instead he didn't make the meeting because he was fucking Ricks and Dizzy's mother.

Dallas was Rick's homeboy that living with them but Dizzy didn't. He moved out when he was about sixteen. Dizzy hated his mother because she was a dope head. Yet all the men loved her cause she had a fucking body that wouldn't wait.

Her body and drug habit got their father killed in a drug sale that she set up it. Dizzy never forgave her for that shit. He moved out about two years after that happened never looking back.

Dallas planned on making the meeting, he got caught up. He had been fucking the woman for a while. She was letting him stay with them for free. Then she started asking for drugs when Dallas gave her that she wanted the dick too.

She heard the young bitches in her hood bragging about him. Dallas fucked her he never told his boy. Now thinking back on it Dallas know that he was a

stupid ass young nigga.

Then word got back to Dallas that

the drop he missed had gotten Ricks

busted. He didn't understand how Ricks

got caught. Dallas knew that whoever

was onto them was coming for him next.

Ricks decided that he would dime

Dallas out. Hoping that would bring back

some of his manhood that was lost. When

got the news about his mom and his boy.

Dallas knew the nigga would bitch

up and dime him out. He left on the first

thing smoking the next day. All he took

with him were two duffle bags with three

hundred thousand dollars and the clothes on his back. Then he headed for St. Louis, MO.

When he touched down in the Lou the first little sexy bitch he bumped into was named was Keshia. She asked him who he was; a duffle bag boy? The statement made him laugh at the pretty face. That was hanging around the bus station. That's when the idea to be just what she called him came.

Now that Ricks bitch ass is a cop he had a hard on for trying to take Dallas down. Little does he know Dallas only looks like the boss of all this shit; he really isn't.

Jay had picked Nisha up before they went to the meeting at Dallas's place. They both jumps back in the whip heading to the airport as ordered. Jay has been unusually quit.

Nisha wondering why but she doesn't bother to ask because she has her own shit on her mind. Jay has been bugging because for the last two weeks a black Range Rover has been following her everywhere she went.

At first she thought it was cute. She wasn't tripping off of it because she know that she is untouchable. Jay was able to get someone to follow the car that has been following her.

She doesn't know the name that is registered to the car. That's she when she became leery of what is taking place. Jay kept the numbers sure as shit it is always the same truck.

Jay beginning to become pissed because she wishes the muthafucka would confront her like a man. Not follow her around like a coward. Then she could properly air their ass out because she always carrying heat.

Even when she is with Q she is strapped but he doesn't know it. That isn't his business she plays it safe at all time.

The muthafucka has to have some kind of balls because he followed her to the meeting at the warehouse. Jay starts to inform Dallas about what is taking place then she decided against it. This isn't anything she can't handle.

Jay know that she doesn't have time to handle it at this very moment. Mr. Black Range Rover is going to get his for sure. Now the bastard is following her to the airport. She know that whoever it they are trying to find the right time to move on her.

Jay always covered. The muthafuckin stalker doesn't know there will never be a right time. He is playing with his fucking life whether he know it or not. As soon as she gets back she plans to put an end this shit.

Cash is becoming more and more impatient with Jay. He has been following her around. Ever since the night he seen her eating with her girls. This is one of the most known important woman that he ever known. He doesn't understanding the way she moves. The woman Jay made him think she was. Isn't the woman he has been following for weeks now. He can't catch her by herself for nothing in the world. Even though he should be trying to kill her ass.

Cash has no plans to hurting her. All he wants to do is ask her why. How could she do him this way? After all they shared together.

Cash loves Jay no matter how much money was taken from him. If he can prove that her love is real, it would be worth the loss. Love is more valuable to him. Jay is the first woman that came into his life. Changing it for the better and worse.

Jay taught him in a blink of an eye the material things can be snatched away from you. She also taught him that love conquers all, because her love conquered him.

Chapter 29

Cash following her wondering where she is heading now. As he follows her he has Poetic Justice by Kendrick Lamar playing. That is his song Jay is the cause of it. *"She could get it,"* his mind tells him.

Cash relationship with Venom is non-existent. She has been treating him like shit. Ever since he clowned her the night he first spotted Jay.

Cash didn't mean to but what he had been looking for was sitting right in his face. As beautiful as the last time he seen her. Now he not getting any pussy from her he barely able to smell or lick it. Venom is not the bitch to treat as second best.

She already has to deal with shit from her twin sister's crew because everyone worships the ground Vicious walks on. Venom loves her sister but hated the power she has. There is no way she is going to allow her man to put another bitch before her.

Cash isn't even allowed to spend the night in her home. When he is in town the nigga is hotel bound. He was pissed at first then he put his focus back on Jay. She is the woman that has his heart.

Venom was a nice fill in once he spotted Jay. Venom time expire from the looks of things he is never going to be able to get to Jay. He watches her pull into the airport. Even there she is not alone.

Jay has guards that carrying her bags and shit. Cash is beginning to think the woman that stole his heart is more powerful than she ever let on. That has his mind fucked up because he realized that trying to get close to her could cost him his life.

Cash money is back to where it was when Jay met him. Now that he is working the South as a part of Vicious team money is not a problem. He is the man to know in his hood again. Things are looking great for him. Cash still has to look into Jay eyes one last time to see what they say.

Is she really as cold as she looks? When he watch her from this distance. She is too beautiful to be living this dangerous life. Cash wishes she would allow him to change her world. So she could be the sweet woman God made her to be. Cash watches Jay disappear into the airport wondering where she would land next.

Duffle Bag Bitches 2

Zane, Nisha, and Jay arrives in Manhattan in no time because things has change for their crew over the course of a few short months. They are no longer flying first class. They are now in their own private plane.

That Dallas had bought for the crew. He actually bought two; one for the crew flying in and out of town. The second one for the new rescue team. that is on deck ready to save the lives of fallen soldiers.

The planes where named DBB Luxury and DBB Emergency. The crew isn't shocked that the plane are name after the women on the team. That's how Dallas rolls; ladies first.

The Four Points by Sheraton Manhattan in SoHo is where the crew staying. Shit looking up for them Jay has to speak on it,

"Aye Z this shit looking better every day right my nigga?" She smiles at how her life has changed.

"Damn right sis I told you to stop calling me Z." He shakes his head at her. Zane doesn't know what is up with people having nickname he is Zane.

"Whatever Z! What the hell is wrong with me calling you Z?" Jay looks at him crazy waiting for him to respond.

"Cause!" Jay is getting on his nerves already. They had just gotten there.

"Cause what nigga?" Jay know that she is working his nerves she doesn't care.

"Why the fuck black people especially Saint Louis people. Got to give a muthafucka a nickname?" Zane asks her pissed off about the shit.

"Cause that's what we do. It's just a way to add a little swag to your punk ass name." Jay is trying to convince him.

"Hell I was born with swag. Don't need a nickname for that. Zane suits me just fine love." Jay and Nisha shakes their heads because they know that Zane on his bullshit today.

They head to the elevator to get to their rooms. Nisha is glad to be first one out of the gate this time. It meant so much to her to make Dallas know that she is capable of doing the job. That she originally proved she could do.

When she got down with his team.
Nisha fucked up last time but not this
time around. She is going to get her
respect this time. Nisha going harder
than ever before. As they exit the elevator
Zane points to the girl's room. Than
heads to his before entering his room he
yells, "Nisha keep your ass in the room
until ordered to leave. I would hate to see
you dealt the same hand this go around."
Zane shakes his head at her simple ass.

Nisha is pissed behind the
statement Zane made. She is the one who
caused everyone to question her. Now is
her chance to change that.

Chapter 30

Dizzy and Jasmine are supposed to still be back home in the Lou. That's not what happened though her and Dizzy left out on the road. Shortly after the other three headed out to the airport. Shannon is the only one still in the Lou at this moment.

Jasmine has to call her husband to explain that she has to leave early. She know that he is going to be pissed. There is nothing she can do at this moment. She doesn't even have a bag packed.

Jasmine dials his number. Thinking she might as well get the shit over with now. The phone ring a few times Korey picks up.

"Hey boo." He is in a great mood . Jasmine is about to fuck that up.

"Hey Daddy I am calling you to tell you that I have to leave early. The boss ordered it." She states causing him to breathe hard.

"The boss? I am your fucking boss! Not some bitch ass nigga that y'all fucking think is a Don or some bullshit!" Korey is not only pissed he sick of the bullshit. Dallas is not going to run his house or family.

"Korey we already talked about this shit. Why you being extra?" Jasmine know damn well why he is tripping. She asks that stupid shit for nothing.

"Bitch I am not in the mood for this shit. I got you and that little fucking crew of yours. I am gonna put an end to this nigga running my fucking house like it's cool. When it's not." Korey know that he crossed the line calling Jasmine out of her name. At this point he doesn't care.

"Bitch? Really? You gone disrespect me like that muthafucka?" Jasmine is pissed she hangs up before he could respond. No matter what she does she isn't going to be called out of her name for no muthafucka. She gone fix his punk ass for sure.

Jasmine sitting in the rental car with Dizzy mad as hell. He doesn't know what to say. If she was his wife she wouldn't be doing this shit. Even if he had to tie her ass up and keep her in the basement. He wouldn't let her risk her life in this manner. That would just fuck with his manhood too much.

Dizzy asks, "Are you ok?" Jasmine

nods yeah. She really wants to cry but

she doesn't.

Dizzy has dropped a fucking bomb

on her so big. That she has to help him or

he is going get himself killed. Jasmine

can't let that happen he is family at the

end of the fucking day. She is blown away

about him being a fucking cop. Most of

all by how she ends up helping him.

Jasmine will never understand why

she agreed because she can't stand pigs.

Then to top the shit off her husband is

livid with her. She doesn't even know if

she will have a husband when she gets back.

Jasmine damn sure gambling with her life. Her heart tells her that Dizzy is a pig on a leash. That's dying to break free of the life he is forced to live all these years. Someone is walking his ass like a dog. Its time to put an end to that shit.

Dizzy wants out that's where Jasmine comes into play. Right now she is the only person he trusts. She hold all of the card whether she know it or not.

Dizzy merges onto I-55 N/I-70 E toward Chicago/Indianapolis. Jasmine is sitting there thinking about this long ass ride, and her husband. She can't turn back now Jasmine is in too deep.

If Korey would respect that shit would be fine. Jasmine had to ask exactly how long the trip will taking, "Dizzy how long is this fucking trip?" She has to know because all this fucking riding isn't for her.

"Fourteen hours I'm gonna try to cut is down to ten. Once the traffic dies down after midnight." He is crazy for trying to shave four hours off a trip. Dizzy plans to drive a hundred miles an hour. Hell he is the police; he will get away if he is stopped.

"You're fucking talking about driving all night nigga? Are you crazy?" Jasmine doesn't know why she even bothered to ask that question. She know that he is.

"Jasmine I bring you with me on this trip. Because I think you're the only muthafucka that won't kill me for being a cop. Trust me like I trust you when I say that I am ready to put an end to this shit." Dizzy let her know his motives for bring her along are good.

"I feel you but you're wrong. I'm the first bitch to kill for being a cop. Because I hate you muthafuckas. The way you told me you lost your family. Allow me have a soft spot for your ass, I hate the pigs a little bit more now than I did before. If a muthafucka killed my family like that I wouldn't know what to do nor how to live." Jasmine let him know this is not because he is safe with her. She loves her family thinks about them every time she gambles her life fucking with the crew for this money.

Dizzy looks at Jasmine to see if she is serious. Her eyes says if he is lying she will kill his ass the moment she finds out.

"Sis I am so ready to get out of this shit."

Dizzy confesses for the first time.

Chapter 31

"The fucking police department! They never done shit to try to find the muthafuckas that killed my family. I know it was all planned out by the last hustler I busted.

The words found on the note in my house were the last words he said to me. Since he killed himself the force feels that they have no leads. They just swept the shit under the rug." Dizzy tells Jasmine.

"What hurt me the most is that everything that little nigga told me about me working for the police is true. They don't give a fuck about me or hard years of work I put in for their sorry ass. After this happened I loss it for a minute. Those muthafuckas fired me.

You hear what the fuck I am saying Jasmine? They fired me for no fucking reason! Didn't even give me the chance to quit on my own. Technically I am not the police, I used to be." Dizzy getting pissed by the second tearing the lines off the highway.

He needs to talk about this. It is time to let this shit go for good. Dizzy can't keep blaming himself for the rest of his life. "If they fired you, why didn't try to get revenge for your damn family? Why are you still working for these muthafucka bruh?" Jasmine ask him.

The questions blew his mind. Jasmine blown her own mind thinking about the situation.

"Who says I am still working for them? I just told I need to handle before we move on the nigga Eric in NY." Dizzy is puzzled with the fact that she is onto him.

"Nigga you think I am going to jump on the muthafuckin highway with you.

Not know what the fuck I am getting into to? Your ass got to be crazy as hell." Jasmine batches.

At first he didn't understand how her and Shannon were sisters. Now he sees it she is fucking insane too he loves it. *"Too damn bad she's married,"* he thinks to himself.

"Fuck it! Now you know. Now what?" Dizzy is testing her to see how much she know. See if he can call her bluff or shut her the fuck up.

"I don't know shit! You better start speaking now or forever hold your peace."

Jasmine shows him the chrome nine that she has with her. Dizzy gets tickled because for the bitches on his crew to dress so sexy.

They carried some serious heat that's hard to hide. Somehow they pulls it off. "You gonna shoot me?" Dizzy asks as he smiles at her.

"Do you have a death wish?" Jasmine cocks the hammer. For the first time she realized how handsome Dizzy s.

Dizzy can't believe this shit. He thought he was out of harm's way. Until he could make this shit right. That is not the case he is in the car with the craziest bitch of all time. That's about to shoot him while he is driving a car she is in.

"Girl what the fuck is wrong with you? I thought you were on my side. Now you want to pulling this bullshit." Dizzy is pissed now thinking maybe Dallas has set him up.

"Boy fuck what you talking about! You better give it to me raw. I am not on teams with anyone that works with the pigs. You can take me and my whole fucking team down." Dizzy feels where she is coming from

He was about to tell her everything when his phone rings. Speak of the devil; Ricks is calling at the wrong time. He has been calling while he was in the meeting at Dallas's house. Dizzy know then that this shit was way out of order.

Dizzy decides to put this nigga on speaker phone. So the crazy lady holding the gun can hear the details for herself. "Hello." Dizzy know that Ricks is pissed. He hasn't been taking his calls for the past few days.

"Don't hello me muthafucka. Where have you been?" Ricks bitches like they are lovers instead of brothers.

"I had a fucking meeting with the boss and team!" Dizzy isn't in the mood for this shit. He has a long drive ahead of him.

"Fuck that nigga! Dallas ain't no muthafuckin boss. We will see how much of a boss he is when his ass sitting behind bars." Ricks instantly became pissed. Thinking how this nigga is living a king's life he is barely making it.

"Man chill the hell out." Dizzy is getting sick of his obsession with Dallas.

"I don't have time to chill out. Are you in New York yet? We need to get a move on things." Ricks is running out of the time his boss gave him. He doesn't care about the case on Dallas. This is Rick's bullshit that he is wasting too much valuable police time on.

"Some of the crew is there. I told you; you'll get your hands on the crew but not Dallas. He is untouchable." Dizzy wants to rub that fact in his face.

"Fuck that nigga! He ain't shit. Once I get my hands on his little crew. I will tear them apart they will hand him right over to me." Ricks is excited about his little plan that he is working on. He wants to have Dallas locked up. So he could get him killed in prison.

"Ricks I am just making sure that you know the deal. We done after this I can move on with my life." Dizzy us tired of being bossed around by this clown.

"Are all the member's males?" Ricks asks because he doesn't know much about the crew.

"No. There are four females known as the Duffle Bag Bitches." Dizzy is warning him yet he too stupid to get the hint.

"Good they will be the easiest to break." Ricks smiles to himself thinking. That he might even get to have his way with one if not all four.

"Yeah right." Dizzy laughs hanging up before he could speak again.

Jasmine sits there listening wondering how this shit will play out. It is wild that he has this sorry ass brother to begin with. The man is trying to get him to do just to bring down Dallas is insane.

Jasmine can tell by Dizzy's tone of voice that he wants out. She has to be sure with this thing because shit can turn on your real fast. Look at the shit Jay pulled last mission. The thought of the shit blows her mind because her own best friend fooled her.

"Are you really ready to get out this shit Dizzy?" Jasmine asks him as she put the gun away.

"Hell yeah! If I wasn't I wouldn't be in this car with your crazy ass girl." Dizzy assures her.

"I mean really sure? Who is that cat you were just talking to?" Jasmine needs to see if this man is important to Dizzy.

"Ricks is my brother." Dizzy says. The way he said it is something missing from the statement.

"Can you kill him if needed?" Jasmine know this question will give her the missing piece to the statement he made.

"In a heartbeat." Dizzy words are so damn cold it pierces her heart. Just what the doctor ordered for her to make her next move before Dallas killed both their asses.

Chapter 33

Zane, Nisha, and Jay has been in New York for a whole day now. They been chilling, shopping, and eating out, nothing hard as of yet. They were having lunch at Quest when Dallas calls. Zane is saved by the bell because Jay is yelling at him about bringing them here to eat this sorry as food.

He shakes his head at her this why he doesn't really like hood bitches. They act a fool everywhere they go.

Zane answers the phone fussing.

"Excuse me?" Dallas chuckles a little.

"I am having lunch with Nisha and Jay. I am about to kill one of them. You will thank me when I get home." Zane informed him what is taking place.

"Ok then." Dallas laughs because he know that it is hard to get on Zane's nerves. The girls are pushing it.

"What's good in the hood nigga?" Zane moves things right along.

"Details my dude." Dallas says.

"Do tell I am all ears." Zane pulls out a little notepad.

"The nigga Eric will be at the Lexicon Night Club at 226 E 54th St. The three of you are to show your face at the club. He assumes that you're here on business trying to move some weight here. Do you follow?" Dallas always wants his orders followed to the letter.

"I got you bruh this is my job. Keep talking time is money." Zane tells him. Dallas loves the way he is on point with the task at hand.

"Eric won't show up until about 11ish. You know that pretty boy shit. So you guy don't get there until twelve fifteen. Not a minute early. No one

usually comes to this club after him.
That's the reason he goes so late. Eric is
a classy businessman you need to get
your swag up to ten thousand.

Jay and Nisha need to do what they
do best get super sexy." Dallas's mouth is
running full speed. Zane understands it
all.

"I got you Boss. You want me on my
GQ shit you want these bitches dipped."
Zane states in the form of a question.

"Yes sir you got it." Dallas is proud
of him.

"Question." Zane states.

"Shoot I got to go heading into the hospital to sit with Mack." Dallas is at the entrance to the hospital.

"Are we to talk business and numbers or just play shit cool enjoy the party?" Zane needs to know how to move if the nigga pressed him for business info.

"No matter what he asks you about business wise. Never talk about it with him. Tell him you just here to enjoy his city. That you like to make friends before doing business." Dallas a cool ass nigga.

"I am going to make this shit happen my nigga. What's the deadline to wrap this nigga up?" Zane likes to be in and out.

"Monday enjoy your lunch, tell my girls I love them." Dallas ends the call.

Jay and Nisha are staring him down waiting for him to tell them what Dallas said.

Zane begin to eat they both chime "What he say?" They are itching to know.

"Oh he said enjoy your lunch he loves you gals." Zane smiles at them. They know that he would share the rest with them later. They don't have any choice but to eat their food.

Zane laughs on the inside. He loves to mess with the girls. He knows it drives them crazy. He also thinks that's why Jay calls him Z. That is the only thing she has learned that works his nerves the way he works theirs.

Dallas entered the room finds Mack sitting up watching television. He is beginning to wonder when this nigga sleeps. Hell he has been in a coma for a few months.

Still Dallas would think with all the therapy this nigga doing that he would need some pain pills. That would knock his ass out.

Mack had become sensitive to movement and scents that he speaks without even looking back.

"What's good Dallas? You bring me some green this time?" He continues to laugh at the television.

"No I didn't you trying to get a nigga like me locked up? How the hell you know it is me anyway?" Dallas asks him.

"It's the way you shuffle your feet when you walk my dude. Also the cologne you have on no one else wears that. Plus, Zane is out of town Roc is on standby." Mack schools his ass. Dallas is thinking damn this nigga on point that's a good thing.

"Nigga if you ever go back in the field you gonna be a monster with that gift." Dallas wishes he could do that shit but that's what laying in a coma does for you.

"If? What the fuck you mean if?" Mack is facing Dallas now he is pissed.

"I am just saying man; you almost died out there. I feel like I owe you a Capo job where you ain't got to do that shit." Dallas didn't think the room was gonna heat up like this today.

"Capo? I ain't no muthafuckin Capo! Give that shit to Zane or Dizzy. I'm gonna be in the field until I die." Mack is so serious no matter how foolish it sounds.

Chapter 34

"I didn't mean to offend you bruh. I thinking you earned it." Dallas is fucked up because he thought Mack would be happy about becoming Capo.

"I didn't earn shit, I lived. If I had died you wouldn't be standing here making me a fucking boss. So miss me with that shit. You don't owe me shit Dallas. I chose this life just like you. I am my own man if or when I die out there.

It will be because the man above punched the clock on me. I am grateful to Roc but he did not save my life. He just got me to the hospital. So don't think now that you have set up this little rescue team. That it means you will not lose people. God makes that call not you Dallas." Mack has to give it to him raw.

"I am sorry man. You're right, if you had died this job would be Zane's. I t let my feelings get in the way. Forgive me cause now that I am looking at you. I am having a hard time forgiving myself. I am not from here you and Zane are all the family I have.

I was just learning to deal with the fact that you were dead. When Roc came into my life." Dallas feels so good getting this shit off his chest.

"How did Roc find you?" Mack asks knowing that Dallas is hard man to get to.

"He didn't really he had some shit going with Laura. Shannon bumped into them later down the line Laura lied about all the shit. Shannon brought her witness to the private meeting I called. That happened to be Roc we cleared up the shit that had taken place with Laura.

That's when he told me that he had something he wanted to show me. We ended up here." Dallas can't believe the way shit has happened.

"Yeah I schooled him on Laura's ass but he was sweet on the bitch. Roc kept trying to drill me on how I knew her. I told him that I couldn't tell him that. She was for damn sure bad business. As it seems maybe she isn't; she got him to where he needed to be." Mack stated.

"Yeah she damn sure did that." Dallas confirms.

"How is shorty anyway? Did she get her shit together?" Mack asks hoping that she did.

"She dead." Dallas states.

"Really man? I didn't think you would do shorty like that." Mack has seen Dallas let other bitches off the hook for way more. He knows living with the type of money they make is far worse than death.

"I didn't kill her." Dallas states.

"Who did?" Mack is confused because he knows that people don't fuck with Dallas's women. No matter if it is right or wrong. They tell Dallas let him handle that.

"Shannon did." Dallas smiles not that he wanted Laura dead.

"My sister." Mack laughs because he should have known.

"Yup." Dallas laughs.

They are chilling watching TV and eating pizza that Dallas ordered when Dallas's phone rings, "State your business and get off my phone." Dallas tells the caller. Mack laughs because this nigga is too cool for him

"You think you hot shit don't you?" the caller asked.

"I am flattered but I am not into niggas. So tell me what you need." Dallas is not in the mood for the bullshit." He

trying to enjoy his pizza.

"Nigga I told you if you get my wife

hurt I am killing you didn't I?" Korey is

pissed.

"You again. Is your wife hurt? She

should be home safe with you pimping."

Dallas is wondering why dude is tripping.

Most of all why he is calling him.

"Jasmine not home with me. She

told me that you sent her out early. I am

sick of you running my fucking house."

Korey barks because he feels the nigga is

playing games.

"I didn't order her to do a damn thing like that. I am going to find out where she at. Because now it seems likes she's calling shots. I am left to take the blame." Dallas is pissed.

"You better find her before I do." Korey hung up.

Chapter 35

Dizzy is rolling on the highway. They were making great time. Jasmine refused to drive so Dizzy is on his own. The nigga had Five Hour Energy on deck for get sleepy.

He isn't too worried about that because he doesn't sleep much normally. Jasmine is sound asleep in the backseat. Dizzy can see her in his rearview mirror. She is a beautiful woman.

He could tell that she is a handful that he doesn't want. If he ever has another man's woman in his life she will have to be soft and feminine. Woman nowadays are too hard act as if they have balls bigger than most men. Dizzy doesn't find that sexy at all.

Jasmine's phone begins to ring. She made a call before falling asleep. She hears the phone picking up on the second ring

"Talk to me." Dizzy shakes his head because he doesn't think a woman should answer the phone like that.

"Hey Jasmine! What fuck did I do to deserve this call?" Kim asks her. Kimberly Burns Pierson is one of NY's finest. She doesn't take any shit either because she didn't have to. She has been a part of New York's police department for more than thirty years.

Kim know all the ins and outs she isn't to be fucked with either. She has sent so many niggas to Ryker's the shit is funny. She is about five-foot-tall, honey blonde hair that she kept feathered to the T. She is thick with an hourglass shape. She has three sons at forty-seven years young she is pushing a Cadillac CT4. Yes; she is bad in every way.

"Kim you that bitch. I love you so I got to call fuck with you every now and again." Jasmine is bullshitting Kim she knows it.

"Get the fuck out of here bitch tell me what's really hood as you muthafuckas would say in the Lou." Kim teases her. As she stands outside the police station smoking a blunt.

"Damn you know me too well bitch. I need a favor." Jasmine tells her.

"What the fuck is new?" She is forever in Jasmine's debt. Due to a bust that she was on here in New York. Jasmine was here setting the nigga up not know that he was going get busted while she was there.

During the bust Kim was almost killed. Jasmine saved her life by killing the shooter. Kim didn't know Jasmine but after that Jasmine become very good friends. Whenever wild young lady needs her to pull some strings she will.

"Ricks is the name." Jasmine tells her.

"What about the bastard?" Kim asks.

"He is supposed to raid our mission. I don't need that to happen but that's not enough. He is blackmailing one of my team members that would rather keep his name off the pigs list." Kim laughs because Jasmine always called her when she needs a favor.

"I know Ricks. He is the clown of the department. He used to be a street nigga. He didn't have what it takes to cut it in the streets. So he did a little time in Ryker's while he was in there he started diming niggas out for a chance at a police job when he got out.

That's Ricks in a nutshell. If you don't want me to have him stop the raid. What do you want me to do?" Kim asks.

"Show up to the raid just to be there. Make the call that officer is down the killer has gotten away. You feel me?" Jasmine asks her.

"I feel you I am down because I hate fake ass cops. If this was one of my good men...." Jasmine cut her off because she knows what Kim is saying.

"I know thank you for all the help. See you in about six hours." Jasmine told her.

"Yup." Kim throws the roach then heads back in the building.

Dizzy listens to Jasmine's call he is shocked that she has a pig in her pocket. Not just a cop the cop of all cops Kimberley Burns. He remembers her wonders if she remembers him.

When Jasmine hang up he questioned her, "How do you know Kim?" Dizzy is impressed.

"I saved her life a few years ago. We been tight ever since." Jasmine informs him.

Dizzy is shocked Kim got caught slipping because she is usually always on top of her game. He is glad to know that

Jasmine believes him. She is also well connected. Dizzy doesn't know how but once this all over he will find a way to repay her for her trust. For now, he could only say, "Thanks." Jasmine smiles.

"No worries. Kim is one of the coolest white girls I know. She will take care of us. When the time comes you better be prepared to kill your brother." Dizzy know that Jasmine is not playing games. If he doesn't she will kill them both.

Kim is glad to help Jasmine. That is not an issue. If it isn't for that young woman she wouldn't be sitting in her office today. So it's all love between the two. There is only one thing she never told Jasmine.

When she was younger she traveled to Portland back in her hey days. Kim was on business when she ran up on one of the sexiest pieces of chocolate known to man. Ever since she always had a sweet tooth for chocolate. Kim picked up the phone "Hey Dallas." She spoke in her sexy voice.

"Hey baby long time no see boo." He smiles because this woman is a force to be reckoned with. If he was to ever marry

she would be it but she walks on the

other side.

Chapter 36

Zane has given the ladies all the details that they need for the night. Not too much to do look sexy. That is easy because who does that better than the Duffle Bag Bitches.

Nisha is excited, "I wonder what that nigga Eric looks like." Not that it really matters because he is an undercover fun boy.

"Hell I don't care what he looks like. I just want to know what kind of chips he holding. We are in Manhattan so I know for sure he major."

"Hell yeah. You know Dallas ain't about them nickel and dime stunners. They can keep that little shit." Nisha riding Dallas's dick hoping that one day she would become the bosses bitch.

"I know we better get ready cause time is rolling around." They both looking at the clock it reads ten fifteen. It's most definitely time to put their sexy on.

Zane is across the hall in his suite dripping wet. He just stepped out of the shower so he could get GQ real quick.

He is lotioning his rock hard body when his phone begins to ring. He walks around the room naked looking for his phone. Zane found it in the bathroom.

The phone read Shannon's name he thought he was tripping. He picks up anyway, "Hello." Zane got sexy for a minute.

"Don't fucking hello me." Shannon barks.

"Well what do you say when someone calls your phone?" Zane quizzes her.

"Oh now I am just somebody?" Zane is trying to figure out who she thought she was.

"You're Shannon right?" Zane asks.

"Muthafucka you know who I am!" Shannon is pissed because he is playing games.

"No who are you?" Zane wants to hear the response she would give.

"Your woman!" Zane has been waiting to hear those words for weeks now. Yet he is not about to allow Shannon to think she could just pick him up and put him down when she sees fit.

"No you're not." Zane says calmly.

"Yes the fuck I am." Shannon is just going make a nigga be with her. No matter how much Zane loves her. She isn't going to ever move like this again once she gets him back.

"You broke up with me called the wedding off. How do you know that I haven't moved on?" Zane hasn't moved on. He wants to make her think about her actions.

"Oh so you ask bitches to marry you then move on like that? Ok cool." Shannon is mad because she did this to herself.

"No I asked a woman to marry me. She said yes, then shortly after she called it off. So what was I supposed to do lay down and die?" Zane can't believe her balls.

"No! So that's why that bitch called you. When you were leaving the meeting. She must be treating you right because you are dipped and happy." Shannon wants to hear his answer.

"Shannon who calls me is not your business after you dumped me. I got a party to go to. I'll see you when you get to New York boo." She is about to say something but he hung up already.

Jay is dresses to kill in a combo by Alyce 5497 Black Label. The top features a fitted bust and waist embellished with a lacy design along both the top and bottom. The skirt is a solid color with a broad striped pattern in the material.

The shoes are nude chunky peep-toe platform shoes with bow details by Allure April. She tops it all off with a nude glitter finished clutch with a glitzy rhinestone closure.

Nisha isn't half stepping tonight either. She wearing a strapless cocktail dress with a sequined panel by La Femme. It had a shoulder-baring bowtie neckline. The center inset is encrusted with the prismatic twinkle of sequins. Tiny sideline tucks create a stellar fit.

Duffle Bag Bitches 2

Her shoes game is insane with shimmering fuchsia peep-toe sling back shoes. A fuchsia sequined party clutch set shit off. Zane told the ladies to meet him in the lobby at the bar at eleven fifteen. They are having Cosmopolitans when he comes walking in.

They notice when he asks, "Would you lovely ladies care to join me in my limo?" The boy looking sharp. A black vintage stripe tailored fit Black Label three-piece suit with black wing tip shoes. A men's derby bowler hat has him looking incredible.

It's a beautiful white color with a stylish feather in the brim. Yes, sir the nigga looks like old and new money for show.

Nisha and Jay could not believe how great he looks. They are smiling from ear to ear at him. Jay snapped a quick picture so she could send it to Shannon later. He laughs "Don't jock me now cause we running late. You know the boss hates that." The women agreed allowing Zane to lead the way to the limo.

Duffle Bag Bitches 2

The arrives at Lexicon Night Club at twelve on the nose. It's great a few people were hanging outside. Still hoping to get in but after midnight you have to have already RSVP' or major cake.

The limo pulls up to the entrance the driver gets out opening the door. The trio exits the car as the standbys watch in amazement.

Chapter 37

Zane walks up to the guard whispered in his ear because the music is so loud it could be heard outside. "The name is Zane." The guard remembers that name because it's reserved with a twenty-five-thousand-dollar tab.

He is glad to bring the man and his guests in, "Right this way sir." The guard walks them to VIP their table next to Eric.

Eric watches as Zane and the ladies took their seats. He knows that is the man he supposed to be doing business with because no one other than him came in this late. He is loving the swag that Zane has.

Eric is not wild about the women hanging around. He watches as Zane pours champagne for the women as they giggle and laugh with each other. Eric very rarely leave his chair to approach anyone. This nigga from the Lou had him open Eric whole crew know it the moment his feet hit the floor.

Zane watches the nigga watching him. He hates fun boy ass niggas especially the ones that have the hots for other niggas. When Dallas first asks Zane to do this he almost killed Dallas's ass.

Than Dallas let him know that all he has to do was play the big man reel old boy in. He knows that it would be easy fucking with a fun boy.

Eric taps Zane's shoulder, "Well hello Zane." Eric smiles.

The tone of the nigga's voice makes Zane's skin crawl. Whoever doesn't know that he is gay has to be a damn fool. "What's good with you pimping?" Zane looks like he is heading to a photo shoot for GQ. His vibe says he is gangsta.

"So are you enjoying Manhattan? I would love to show you the city. As we talk business because I see right now we have company." Eric gave Nisha and Jay the evil eye. They almost spit out their champagne in laughter.

"There's nothing we will talk about. That can't be talked about in front of these ladies. This is Jay and Nisha." Zane introduces him to the girls. Eric looks at two women as if they are shit on the bottom of his shoe.

"I didn't know that. I like to only do business with my friends so this might not work." Eric is pissed thinking that he would never have Zane alone to make his move.

"Why do I have to be your friend?"
Zane looks at him knowing the ocean
blue eyes would fuck with this nigga's
head.

"Fuck me." Eric thinks but his
mouth says, "You can come to my home
tomorrow night for dinner." Eric is
excited thinking about it.

"Dinner huh?" Zane asks.

"Why not?" Eric flirts.

"What time?" Zane is ready to get rid
of his ass.

"Nine." Eric smiles.

"You always eat that late?" Zane is playing games with him. Jay gave him dap under the table.

"No! You're special." Eric is dick riding.

"Yes I am." Zane agrees.

"Well I'll see you tomorrow night." Eric is about to rub his shoulder. When Nisha caught his hand "Zane doesn't like to be touched unless he asks you to. We gave you one pass bit no one gets two." She shut his ass down.

Eric heads back to his table mumbling, *"Bitch."* He is pissed.

The trio ate, laughed, and danced enjoying the beautiful night as Eric watched. In amazement he knows if Zane is the kind of man that could have two women that loved him. He is the kind of man he wants to make love too and do business with.

Chapter 38

Shannon is set to leave on her flight. She is packed in the car heading to the airport. She has a lot of shit on the mind. Mostly the talk she had with Zane. He is right she has no right to walk in and out of his life.

As she please Shannon know that she should have taken time to think the issue over before calling it off.

If Shannon could turn back the hands of time. She wouldn't have called things off. Now that he has moved on she doesn't know if she can handle it. The worst part is that she has no one to talk to about all of this. Jay and Nisha are handling business. Jasmine is nowhere to be found. Korey doesn't even know where she has gone.

Shannon wants Zane back but she doesn't know if she is going be able to get him back. She can tell by the way he spoke to her. That was done out of hurt more than anything.

Shannon couldn't be mad about it because she caused the hurt. Now it's time for her to do whatever it takes to get the man she loves back. Manhattan needs to be ready for Shannon.

Duffle Bag Bitches 2

Dallas wake up with his mind fucked up after the call that he got from Kim. He went out got drunk because the shit is too much to process. This is not what he signed up for. What the hell does he think comes with the job. It sure as hell isn't a 401k plan or pension.

Dallas is glad to find out that Dizzy is not a cop anymore. He has not been one for many years. He feels sorry that the nigga is Rick's brother.

Now Ricks bitch ass giving his brother a hard time blackmailing him and shit. Dallas wishes that he could kill

Ricks bitch ass himself. What Kim told him it's all about to come to an end.

Dallas e trusts her words more than anyone in this world. She informs him as to how she came up with this info. Dallas had to laugh because that girl was everywhere getting money. He is shocked that they never tried to get at him. He doesn't floss so he is kind of hard to spot.

Dallas is kind of pissed that Dizzy hadn't come to him. Then again he couldn't blame the man. Because he was ready to put the nigga in a body bag up to this point. Dizzy decides to put his trust in Jasmine.

Dallas is glad the girl is loyal to their whole crew not just him. That speaks volumes to him.

Dallas has to get his shit together because today is the day. That everything is supposed to go down. The crew would be back home on Monday morning as planned. He has to make sure the new headquarters up and running for the payday meeting.

Dizzy and Jasmine made it to New York in ten hours. He checks them into a Motel 6 so that Jasmine could freshen up and get some rest. She has been bitching about not been able to do her womanly bodily duties. Dizzy is glad that her ass is not sound asleep after all the shit she had him go get from Walmart.

He is sitting in his room thinking about his wife. How much he misses her when Ricks knocks on his room door.

Dizzy opens the door Ricks walks in like he the shit. Doesn't even bother to say hello begin drilling him. "What time do we move in?" Ricks is too happy.

"I don't know yet because I just got here. My crew is in Manhattan in a penthouse suite." That nigga has to be crazy if he thinks Dallas's family would be in some shit like this.

"Your crew in the penthouse huh? Well they're about to be in the jailhouse thanks to you." Boasts as if Dizzy isn't his brother.

"Man fuck you!" Dizzy is pissed; he could kill this nigga right now.

"What?" Ricks can't believe that this nigga is flexing like that.

"I said fuck you I mean it too! After this shit is over don't contact me any fucking more. because I am tired of this sorry ass life. You can have this shit. I want a family I am going to get one. You won't be a part of it either." Dizzy finally told him how he feels.

"So you want to keep living this life working for a punk ass thug like Dallas?" Ricks doesn't understand him.

"I have made and saved more money working for that sorry ass punk. Than I did working for this sorry ass force and crooked ass cops. Dallas has been more of a brother to me than you ever fucking have Ricks." Dizzy is fed up. Ricks know he has pushed him too far but it was too late to let up now.

"Fine after I get Dallas I am out of your life. You will never have to worry about your crooked ass brother calling you again for shit." Ricks is hurt that Dizzy feels this way.

"No after this mission you raid I am done. I don't give a fuck if you ever get Dallas or not. I always told you that it was a gamble. The man's hands stay clean. Unless the crew members give you something your case on him is dead." Dizzy got real with him because it was becoming too fucking much.

"I call the shots here not you. You will be done when I say that you're done. You got that muthafucka?" Rick thought that would work.

"Muthafucka I call the shots for me. You can lock me up now. That's all you will have an insane ass ex-cop that they will let out in a few months. So tell me how you want to do this." Dizzy dials nine one one all he has to do is press send.

"Be easy; get me the crew and I am out of your life for good. They will get me Dallas for sure." Ricks has to make himself believe that. It's the only way he would be able to sleep tonight.

"That what I thought muthafucka. Now get out my room wait for the call." Dizzy is over this shit.

Jasmine hears his door open for the second time. She opens her door to see Dizzy standing outside watching a strange man get in his car.

"Who is that bruh?" she asks.

"My brother. I was just taking out the trash. Now go back to sleep because we to head to Manhattan soon." Dizzy is sexy when he bossy.

"Sure thing Daddy!" Jasmine closed her door to get some much needed sleep.

Dizzy laughs at her but once he was in his room he broke down crying for the loss of his wife, child, job, life, and mind.

He thanks God for allowing him to know Dallas and his crew. The love they have given him over the years is what keeps him alive.

Dizzy had thought of killing himself many times because he has nothing to live for. Today he knows that is far from the truth. He has a real family that loves him. A second chance to love again if he came across the right woman. He is ready to live life. He just has to get through this mission back to the Lou.

Chapter 38

The knock at the door throw Nisha and Jay's conversation off. When Jay opens the door Shannon is standing there, "What's hood bitches?" she smiles.

Shannon is looking a little thick today. "Damn bitch you getting thick leaving me behind." Nisha teases as she hugs Shannon.

"I'm doing a little something. You know a bitch be eating and shit." Shannon jokes glad to be around her girls. She is glad to be off that long ass flight more than anything she was ready for action.

"I see." Jay agrees.

Shannon put her bags down asks, "What room's Zane in?" she needs to talk to him.

"He's across the hall girl." Nisha tells her.

Shannon turns on her heels heading out the door. She needs to see his face. Shannon wants to kiss him. She just needs to see how lucky she could get. She knocks at his door.

When Zane opened it she knew that he would be naked or wrapped in a towel. Thank God he has the towel on because if he didn't she would have dropped down sucking his pretty dick right there.

Shannon loves this man. She can tell by the look on his face that he is shocked it's her that had knocked on his door.

"Hello Ms. Lady." Shannon loves when he called her that.

"Can I come in?" She asks.

"Nope." Zane wants to let her in. But he is not her play toy she needs to know that.

"Really?" Shannon can't believe her ears.

"Yes. Is there something you need Shannon?" He is killing himself she has to learn.

"I need to know what time we're gonna make the move on ole boy." She lies.

"I meet him at nine by eleven you guys should be breaking in to set shit off. It's very simple you have done this before. Girl quit acting like a rookie." Zane know that he is blowing her mind.

"Cool. You right; I'm better than you at this. I don't know why the fuck I bothered to ask you." Shannon shoots back it hurts.

Zane watches her walk away. She is getting thick as hell he wants to call her back.

He should tell her he is playing and then throw her on the bed. Eat her pussy likes she loves him to. He has to close the door because he doesn't want to chance her looking back seeing his dick rock hard.

Dizzy and Jasmine are back on the road heading to Manhattan. Tonight is the time when shit is going to hit the fan. Jasmine has talked to Kim everything a go. Dizzy is glad to, he needs peace of mind.

Dizzy wishes he would have been able to chill in that plush ass hotel. That isn't going to happen this trip; maybe next time. Dallas is already on to some nigga in Vegas.

They made it to the hotel about seven. A few hours before all the shit about to jump off. Jasmine went to the girl's room. As Dizzy taps on Zane's door.

He hoping that it isn't Shannon again. Zane doesn't think he would have it in him to turn her away again.

When he opened the door this time he is wearing basketball shorts. Dizzy staring at him because he knows the love has not been the same between them two lately.

Zane doesn't make shit any better. "Oh it's just yo ass." Zane isn't in the mood to be sharing a room with Dizzy. When he doesn't know if he is a cop or not.

"It's good to see you too family." Dizzy know what he is on.

"I wish I could say the same about you." Zane states coldly.

"I am trying to figure out why you can't. I haven't done shit to you the last time I checked my dude." Dizzy is not in the mood for this bullshit.

"Man kill that bullshit." Zane is getting pissed because he is playing dumb.

"No you cut it! You never came to me like a man. Nigga speak on what is on your chest. You walking around assuming shit." Dizzy fucked with his manhood.

"You right! The question is are you the cops?" Zane needs to know.

"I used to be." Dizzy tells the truth.

"What the fuck you mean you used to be?" Zane is hot.

"Before I came to the Lou I was a cop in Portland, OR. After one of my busts got my wife and daughter killed. I lost my mind they kicked me off the force. I relocate to Lou after that." Dizzy feels so good letting all this shit out.

"Wife and kid? Who are you nigga?" Zane is confused.

"The same nigga that you grew to love with a past." Dizzy gave him the real business.

"Well if you used to work for them. Why are you back helping them take down your family?" Zane doesn't understand that.

"I am being blackmailed by my brother that is a cop. I am here in New York to an end to this shit. No matter if the crew believes, trusts, or Dallas kills me I am ending this shit tonight for me. I hope you understand that." Dizzy is fed up.

"I'm sorry family. I believe yo ass. I know you if you were crooked. If had blown your cover you would have aired my ass out right, there." Zane know that.

"You willing to risk your life for that?" Dizzy asked.

"Ain't that why we in this hotel now? Risking our necks for each other so we can live well one day?" Zane counters him.

"That's why I am here; for the love of my crew." Dizzy assures him.

"Me too." Zane agrees.

"One love, One heart, One life!" Dizzy shares the motto Zane, Dallas, Mack, and he shared when they first started out.

Zane smiles, "My nigga!" he hasn't heard that shit in so long it takes him back to a good place. He hugs Dizzy, "I'm glad you're not a cop. It would be hard to kill you." Zane means that because he loves this nigga.

"You damn right cause I ain't no easy kill nigga." Dizzy stuck his chest out.

"Oh, is that right?" Zane steps back admiring his boy.

"You know it! I am Dizzy Body Bangs you know about me family." Dizzy smiles.

"My nigga!" Zane laughs with him because he is the one to give Dizzy that name. After one mission where Dizzy killed ten niggas on his own.

The love is back the mission is right. It is time to go get this money then head back home to enjoy life.

Chapter 39

205 E 59Th St, New York, NY 10022
is the address that Eric gave Zane to
meet him at. Zane know the nigga is
holding because the condo he lives in ran
for over a million a month.

Eric is not really a hustler come to
find out. He is a rich kid from a powerful
family. Trump is Eric's last name but
since he is part black the world knows
nothing about him.

The money keeps him quiet. Zane is
wondering why Dallas had him to bring
his laptop with him. Now that he has the

run down on Eric's family he knows this wouldn't be a cash and carry more of a transfer.

Zane walks up to the door dressed in ash grey Kenneth Cole from head to toe. Eric opens the door; he stood six foot five, with caramel skin tone, jet black deep waves, and a muscular build. The nigga has no reason in the world to be a fun boy.

He a major stunner. His ego about to get hurt and his pockets about to get short fucking with Zane. The nigga doesn't even see it coming. He so head over heels with Zane.

"Eric tries to greet him with a hug. Zane cut him off by asking, "Didn't my girls tell you I don't like to be touched?" It was more of a warning.

"Forgive me. I am shocked that you don't have the Pitbull in skirts with you tonight." Eric is glad too.

"Yeah they had better things to do. Is that men hugging men is a New York thang?" Zane insulted him twice in one statement.

"Better things to do?" Eric thinks. He is appalled by the statement but he let it go. "No! I just always show affection or love." He smiles.

As Zane steps through the door he says, "Don't show me either because I am not wild about the two." Zane is cold. Eric likes it because he is the one who usually treats people like that.

Zane admires his home. It is a custom design located in a full service condominium. The elegantly converted two bedrooms is an entertainers dream.

A sweeping city views from the 22nd floor. The condo boasts multi-zone central air and heat. A surround sound system plus wireless speakers throughout the whole place. Gas fireplace, ten foot ceilings, two private balconies, washer and dryer, state of the art windows, and wide plank teak floors.

It is custom designed with exquisite woods thoughtfully integrated modern elements. The home features a chef's kitchen with Viking appliances that opens to the great room and dining area.

Duffle Bag Bitches 2

The gracious master bedroom provides the ultimate in comfort, featuring a large marble bath with soaking tub and separate shower. Heated towel rack and a built in television.

The master suite also includes an ample walk-in closet, and bright corner office solarium.

205 East 59th Street is a full service luxury condominium that offers its residents. Twenty-four-hour concierge service, doorman, resident manager, private fifth floor landscaped garden

terrace, fitness center, service pantry to facilitate catered events.

A mahogany outdoor stretching yoga studio, and a puppy park for canine companions. It is at the crossroads of the Upper East Side and Midtown.

Eric glides around the huge condo like he is on cloud nine. The dinner date of his dreams. The nigga doesn't know it that he isn't going to be eating dinner tonight. Zane had already told the crew that once they heard him say *"No more wine for me,"* it's time for them to move in.

Eric came in with two Ralph Lauren home wine glasses "Red, white or you into mixing the two?" Zane hates this nigga.

"Nigga give me some Hennessey I don't do that wine shit. You can drink that." Zane let the thug back out.

"Have it the way you like it sir." Eric sashays out of the room to get the drinks.

He came back with both drinks in his hand ready to make small talk. Zane is all about business.

"So why you want to walk on this side of life that I'm on? You seem to have money." Zane wants to know why the nigga is gambling with his life.

"I need a hobby so I dibble and dabble a little. Nothing too much, don't want to get my hands dirty." As Eric spoke Zane remembers he needed to set up the laptop.

"Hobby huh? Oh yeah can I set up my laptop? You know put on some music. You know if you join my team you will get dirty." Zane assures him.

"Sure set up your music I'm not afraid of getting dirty." Eric states as he pours the both of them their second drink.

The girls are parked in a van a few blocks away from Eric's home. In the back of his building this time they are going to climb the side of the building come in through the skylight.

They could hear the conversation all Nisha could say was, "He is too fine to be gay." Jasmine and Shannon has not seen him so they have no clue what she means.

They both asks. "Is he really?" They both have been wondering from his voice how he looks.

"Girl hell yes." Jay confirms.

Jasmine wonders about Dizzy. She knows that he is safe because he being watched by Kim. Even though he would show up to the scene with Ricks.

Shannon notices that she is not focused. "Sister are you ok?" she asked.

"Yeah baby I am good ready to get this shit over." Jasmine know shit is gonna get real before it is all said and done.

"I am not leaving here without you. So don't worry about shit do what you best at." Shannon loves her sister.

"What's that?" Jasmine needs to know because she doesn't think Shannon think she is good at anything.

"Shooting," all the woman in the car bust out laughing.

Eric is about to pour another drink when Zane informs him, "I could never have another drink. Two is enough liquor makes me lose my head." That nigga is lying through his teeth.

"Oh one more won't hurt; you're a big boy." Eric flirts.

"You know what the hell pour it up. The music is right." Zane sat back down on the couch because he knows the girls are in motion.

Duffle Bag Bitches 2

Dizzy is sitting in a squad car with Ricks letting him know that is the cue for the girls to move. Ricks has two cars and four men with him for this bust. He was shocked when Kimberly Burns Pierson asked to help him with the bust.

She made him think she had run in with Dallas a few years back. But he got away so he welcomed her aboard.

Jasmine is the one that would signal Dizzy to come in by saying "The money is transferred." He will move the police into the war zone.

The girls are climbing up the north side of the condos to the skylight so they could drop down into Eric's condo. Thank God he is on the top floor of the building making this shit so much easier.

The Duffle Bag Bitches carrying duffle bags tonight not for money but for the shotguns with silencers that were in the bags strapped to their backs. The latex bodysuits they wearing compliments their curves. since having to climb the fire escape killed their heel game.

Zane is sitting on the couch facing the skylight Eric across from him. When the glass broke some of it came down on Eric's head. As the girls slid down the rope with faces uncovered and hair flowing in their all black latex suits. It turned Zane on; maybe it was the Hennessey but it doesn't matter what it is time to go to work.

Eric screamed like a damsel in distress, "Don't hurt him he doesn't have nothing to do with this. He from out of town!" Eric is on the floor in a ball.

Nisha grabs him by the collar, "This has everything to do with him. Now get your ass over to the laptop." Eric remembers Nisha's face.

"You bitch." He swings on her. Shannon hit his ass in the back of the head with the shotgun.

"Get to the laptop fun boy wire the half a million. These ladies gonna Swiss cheese your ass." Zane promises.

"I don't have that kind of money." He isn't thinking when he made that statement.

"Nigga you got five minutes to give me what the fuck I came here for, or it's light out for you." Zane cues the girls to pull the guns out.

The four women stands there looking like Zane's Angels with the shotguns aimed at Eric. He looks in each of their eyes seeing the fire that danced in them. It said that killing is easy so it's up to him.

Eric crawls to the laptop. The money isn't worth his life. He just hopes that they wouldn't kill him so he asks, "If I do this will I live?"

"It's only one way to find ain't it? You got three minutes left." Zane let him know.

"Ok I will do it just don't hurt me!" Eric cries as he transferred the money from his account to the new one that Dallas would take it out of the moment it got there. Then close that account.

Duffle Bag Bitches 2

The screen read *"Transfer Successful"* Jasmine read that off. That is the cue for Ricks and his crew to move in. They are already in the stairway when the command for them to move in came. Zane and Jasmine are waiting for Dizzy to give the clue to shoot.

When the door came flying off the hinges Eric crawls under the table not knowing what the hell is taking place. He had been robbed now the police are kicking in his door. He thought his had neighbors called.

The four policemen that Ricks bring along enters first that's when Dizzy yells,

"Shoot!" Ricks smiles because he thought that his brother is talking to the cops. Until he spots four bad bitches with shotguns. Zane opens the window grabbing the rope placed there for the getaway.

The girls begin to spray the place. The shotguns doesn't make the boom that it usually would. They made whisper that couldn't be heard. The sight could be seen. The four men fell before they could even touch the triggers on their guns.

Ricks is not ready for this when Kim yells, "We've got to get in there help those guys!" She ran in the girls know who she is. So they hold their fire.

Dizzy grabs Ricks because the bastard is not trying to go in. When he did he sees Shannon, Nisha, and Jay getting away through the window.

"They're getting away! Shoot them!" He barks.

Dizzy turns to him, "They're gone there's nothing we can do." He looks at Jasmine her gun is still smoking.

"She is still here." Ricks is about to charge her.

"Boom, Boom, Boom!" Those shots could be heard Dizzy looks down at his dead brother, "Yeah she is still here but you're not." He smiles.

"Get out of here you guys send Dallas my love." Kim hugs Jasmine.

They exit the same way their friends had. Kim makes the call.

"Officer down! Hurry I don't think he's going to make it.

Chapter 40

The crew back at the hotel chilling. Dallas has called telling them all great job. That pay day is coming soon. They are glad that no one got hurt this time. That is the highlight of the day.

Shannon is feeling great from the few drinks she had. She stepped to Zane, "I need to talk to you." She is tipsy.

"About what?" he is drunk.

"Us." She said.

"Is there a u?" Zane needs to know.

"Yes." Shannon smiles.

"What you as my girlfriend?" Zane asks. He is not looking for a girlfriend.

"No as your wife and baby mother." Shannon says.

"You pregnant?" Zane got sober really fast.

"Yes." Everyone in the room is shocked.

"Well why the hell are you drinking?" Zane is pissed.

"I was thirsty." Shannon smiles.

"Next time get your thirsty ass some water." He kisses her the room cheers.

After a great night of rest, the crew all heads to the airport. Dallas didn't send the jet because he wants to play things cool with all that has taken place.

The crew is laughing and joking as they wait to board the plane.

All of a sudden the FBI rolls up on them, "Dizzy and Zane." They states causing the two to turn around.

"Yeah." They both chime.

Nisha tip toes off a no one noticed her. As the two Feds begin to arrest the men.

"Hold the fuck up what we do?"

Zane asks.

Before he could respond bombs start going off in the airport. The last one that went off so loud and close they all thought they would be hurt.

Zane is looking for Shannon when he hears a giant BOOM again. Zane begin to scream

"Where is my wife?

She's pregnant!

Where is my wife?"

Duffle Bag Bitches 2

Authors Note

Thanks for the support

Alicia Howard Presents.

Keep reading I will keep writing until we

meet again.

Love,

Alicia Howard

CPSIA information can be obtained
at www.ICGtesting.com
Printed in the USA
LVOW04s1750021216

515533LV00010B/977/P